Love's Silent Song

JUNE MASTERS
BACHER

HARVEST HOUSE PUBLISHERS
Eugene, Oregon 97402

LOVE'S SILENT SONG

Copyright © 1983 by Harvest House Publishers
Eugene, Oregon 97402

Library of Congress Catalog Card Number 83-080875

Trade Paper ISBN 0-89081-378-7
Mass Paper ISBN 0-89081-013-5

Printed in the United States of America.

Dedicated
to
Arlene Cook,
my inspired and inspiring friend!

CONTENTS

PREFACE

There was a saying among the early Oregon settlers which may well hold true today: "Them that wanted to find gold went to California, but them that came to Oregon wanted to find a home." And there are a lot of North-westerners who would make the same claim today. There's a majestic spell about the region—a something indefinable that makes it *home*.

The Oregon Country is beautiful whether seen as autumn wraps a misty shawl over sun-ripened harvests, winter adds a fresh blanket of snow to the lofty peaks, or summer puts on the green girdle—laced with silver streams—that shapes the state into a nature-lover's paradise. But Oregon is best understood in the spring. It is then that azaleas and rhododendrons try to upstage one another and a million meadowlarks burst into song along some of the best of our nation's highways. Yet for a real glimpse of what the land was once like, the setting in which this book was written and a remnant of which remains, seek the back country. There you will find the near-extinct trillium and lady-slipper orchids, the fern-green glades where moss is made, and the gnarled apple trees which descendants of the pioneers declare were planted by the legendary Johnny Appleseed.

Listening to the residents, you will believe, as I came to believe. Inclining an ear to nature, you will find renewed faith. And faith is what **Love's Silent Song** is all about.

But this is not a history book, nor is it a travel folder. It is a gentle, romantic novel, a sequel to **Love Is A Gentle Stranger,** written as it could only be written by one who has lived in the beautiful green corner of God's footstool— one who has seen it through the eyes of the pioneers and has come to love it as they did.

June Masters Bacher

From the Calapooias to the Siskiyous,
The Cascades to the sea,
Comes the history of the Umpqua—
This mighty land!
To say a century—a hundred years—
How long is that
To battle hardship, hunger, death,
And wash newborn babes in iron tears?
How long is that
To free a country, plow it, and hand it down?
Let us review those mystic moments
To portray with heartfelt reverence
Those immortal pioneers—
Those faithful to the Lord Almighty,
Those led in truth by unseen hand,
And salute our flag of freedom,
Symbol of this mighty land.

—From *Umpqua Cavalcade*
Copyright © 1952 by June Masters Bacher

CAST OF CHARACTERS

Chris Beth (Christen Elizabeth Kelly Craig, wife of minister)

Joe ("Brother Joseph," Joseph Craig, minister)

Vangie (Mary Evangeline Stein North, wife of doctor, Chris Beth's half sister)

Wilson ("Uncle Wil" North, doctor)

Young Wil (Wilson's nephew)

Little Mart (Martin, adopted son of the Craigs)

"True" North (Trumary North, infant daughter of Norths—Wilson's stepdaughter)

"Miss Mollie" (Mrs. Malone, wife of the Irish O'Higgin)

O'Higgin (second husband of "Miss Mollie," stepfather of the six children belonging to her late husband)

Nate Goldsmith (self-appointed school board president and chairman of the board of deacons)

Abe and Bertie Solomon (proprietors of the general store)

Maggie Solomon (their daughter)

"Doc Dullus" (retiring doctor)

"Boston Buck" (Indian brave)

1

Spell of the Brooch

Dobbin's loud neigh from behind the cabin broke the tranquility of the afternoon. Another horse must be approaching. A first caller? Careful not to awaken little Mart, Chris Beth tiptoed to the front window.

How ridiculous to be apprehensive! Mama had seen to it that her daughters grew up receiving guests, making small talk, and serving tea—a practiced skill that became an art when they left Atlanta to attend school in Boston. Ridiculous or not, the sense of nervous excitement persisted. Maybe because the role as lady-of-the-house was so new? No, it was something more. She was sure of that even before spotting the lone rider in the ancient buggy.

Chris Beth, bride of two weeks, turned to look at herself in the bureau mirror for reassurance. She saw the same dark brown hair, braided and wound into a smooth halo, and the same blue eyes—brighter now, aglow. And her cheeks were flushed with what her minister-husband called "that married look." The blush deepened at the intimate phrase, but she felt a little more in control. With cheeks still warm, she moved quickly from the mirror to answer the knock at the door.

"Mrs. Malone!" A flood of relief swept over Chris Beth at sight of her dear friend. "How nice of you to call."

"Wanted to check in on you like." The older woman spoke in her usual warm, no-nonsense manner. "Thought you'd be needin' leaven for sourdough biscuits."

"Indeed!" Chris Beth smiled as she ushered Mrs. Malone inside and pulled Joe's "study chair" forward. "Please sit down and let's have a long chat."

"Not too long. Best I be on hand when O'Higgin and the young'uns bring in the milk. Lots of commotion 'bout then."

Chris smiled again, remembering the general bedlam of Mrs. Malone, her husband O'Higgin, and their six step-children trying to get past Ambrose, the cat, to strain the milk and set it to cool. With O'Higgin's Irish wit, *commotion* was a mild word! Such a warm, loving, hospitable family...Chris Beth wondered when Mrs. Malone would elect to make use of her new husband's name. Their marriage, like her own—and, yes, her sister Vangie's too—was one of the many miracles of this wild and beautiful country. She loved Oregon's every whimsical mood. *Even the flood brought us an orphaned baby to love,* her thoughts raced on.

"Returned this, too." Mrs. Malone fished in her knitting bag.

"This?" Chris Beth repeated, puzzled, as she accepted the small package. "I'm sorry. My mind was wool-gathering—"

The words died on her lips as the wrapping fell to the braided rug. For there inside lay the pearl and sapphire brooch, its gems, like evil eyes, mocking...taunting...threatening....

"Are you all right, child? Why, you're pale like you'd seen a ghost!"

I have, her heart answered, *I have.* Unable to answer, Chris Beth nodded mutely. Fumbling with the wrappings, she managed to get the piece of jewelry out of sight. "I'll put the sourdough in the cooler and make coffee," she murmured, and was grateful that Mrs. Malone took out her knitting instead of offering to help.

In the sanctum of the small kitchen, she went about the comforting routine of setting up the old tea cart as the coffee perked contentedly. But her thoughts went back to the symbol of the brooch...the excitement of first love, the whirlwind courtship with Jonathan Blake...the thrill of engagement parties, wedding plans, and "forever after" dreams...then the heartbreak and humiliation of Jon's broken promises, his plea for freedom, and her emotional death when he confessed that, yes, there *was* another woman. The sun slipped out of the sky at the memories. Long shadows grew and stretched, blotting out the new life she had built here. But, cruelly, the memories persisted, bringing back her escape to the Oregon Country...her stagecoach meeting with Mollie Malone, O'Higgin, and the men she and Vangie would eventually marry. There was Wilson, an aspiring doctor...and her half sister's arrival...and their tearful reunion...and then the awful news that Vangie, her own sister, was to bear Jonathan's child! Oh, the shame of it all!

"Ouch!" Chris Beth almost welcomed the pain she felt when boiling hot coffee splashed onto her hand as she tried to pour it. Almost fiercely she wiped up the spill, unaware that she had used one of her embroidered tea towels.

"But then there was Joe!" she whispered almost prayerfully as she reached for a clean cup. Dear, wonderful Joe, with hands as gentle as his smile and concerned hazel eyes. Joe, whose boyish bronze cowlick looked out of keeping with his big tan frame. Her husband's little lisp when he was under stress endeared him all the more. *And he always smells of good earth*, she thought with a rush of affection for him...for their adopted baby...for Vangie and her new husband Wilson...and all the wonderful friends who had helped her put down roots here.

Mrs. Malone accepted the china cup and looked at Chris Beth above its gold rim. "It was a pretty weddin', wasn't it?"

"It was beautiful!"

So beautiful that it hurt. And the brooch she had forgotten to return to Jonathan, strangely, made it more so! It looked as if it belonged in the blue ruffles of Vangie's wedding gown. The younger girl's eyes had glowed like the sapphires themselves when Chris Beth pinned it there just before their double wedding. Little did Vangie know that it was a gift from the man who had betrayed them both. That's what hurt.

Without realizing that tears were close, Chris Beth spoke. "But it hurts to look back—on the ugly part—"

Mrs. Malone drained her cup before answering. "How well I know," she said quietly as she folded her napkin and pressed it neatly with her hands. "Has its value, though. Like as not, we have to return to the troublin' past before we can find the future."

Then, tucking her knitting into her bag, Mrs. Malone turned tactfully to other matters. But Chris Beth heard little more. Jonathan was dead now. The past was dead too. But her memories were not. They would live on to gnaw away at her life as Mrs. Joseph K. Craig until somehow she broke the evil spell of the brooch and its power over her.

"If I could just come to understand the strange hold it has on me," she said aloud as she put the tea cart back in its corner.

2

New Signs of Life

Chris Beth remembered the brooch as she pulled the flannel robe closely to her body as a protective shield. The unexpected glimpse of it yesterday had chilled her bones to the marrow. In spite of her resolve to put the brooch out of her mind she had slept little, and this morning the cold crept up from her fingertips and encircled her heart. She wished fervently that Mrs. Malone had waited a while to remove the pin from the second-day dress that Vangie had borrowed from her for the wedding. Of course, the generous lady had no way of knowing that a piece of jewelry could bring back all that was hateful and frightening—even threatening—to the new life that she and Vangie had made for themselves here.

But she had best not dally. Joe would be in for breakfast shortly. Checking for needed supplies for the gristmill he and Wilson owned wouldn't take long. He deserved a square meal, a well-groomed wife, and, she thought sadly, one who was in control of the past, happy with the present, and looking forward to the fulfillment of his dreams as a minister of the gospel. That was his life. He had told her so. But she so wanted to put down roots. Could she be jealous of his dedication? The thought was unsettling. Maybe fresh air would help to rid her of such silly misgivings.

Quietly, lest she awaken her little adopted son, Chris Beth opened the bedroom window. New signs of life rushed in to greet her senses.

"Good morning, Lord," she whispered in wonder. Then, thoughtfully, she added, "Forgive me for any unworthy thoughts."

Then in reverence she turned back to the scene around her. March had turned to April, and suddenly spring was born. Wild plums bloomed out in white abandon, and budding sweetbriar softened the angles of every split-rail fence bordering the homesteads of the settlement. Valley women planted early gardens. Their menfolk cautiously sowed spring grain along the warmer slopes and set to work deadening trees for new ground, then turning the rich, mellow soil up to dry in the sun for later corn-planting. Children's squeals of joy and birds' incessant song became "an abolute nuisance" to at least one of the settlers. "Cain't even hear Bossie's cowbell!" Mrs. Malone had complained to Chris Beth when leaving yesterday.

Higher up, in the grazing lands, the Basque sheepherders rounded up the older animals for shearing. Baby lambs grew round and fleecy, and their frolicking bleats blended with the happy sounds of the busy valley below. All was peaceful, beautiful, and comforting—until the memories came back. Chris Beth shivered again, knowing that the chill had nothing to do with the cool of the dew-wet morning.

"And how is my beloved bride?"

The sudden sound of the deep, dearly familiar masculine voice startled her. Joe always removed his muddy boots at the door—"as trained," he teased. So she hadn't heard him enter the room.

"Fine—oh, Joe—"

He drew her close with a little laugh which changed to concern when he felt her trembling. "Think I was going to ambush you? Hardly!"

The strength of Joe's arms around her and the closeness of his body against hers were warmly reassuring. Why, then, was she unable to stop the tremors of her body?

Stroking her hair gently from her face, Joe let his big, capable hand slide down its long, dark cascade over her shoulders. "I should have been braiding it," she murmured vaguely.

"It's beautiful," he said huskily. His hand moved from her hair to her chin, tilting it slightly so he could look into her face. "Something *is* wrong."

When Chris Beth failed to respond, Joe steered her gently to the antique sofa, sat down, and pulled her onto his lap.

But the timing was wrong. This wasn't the time to talk. There were some things she had never discussed with him in their two weeks of marriage or before that. And he had never asked—until now.

Joe's arms tightened about her.

"Sometime—but not now, please," she whispered.

His arms loosened. "I'm sorry." There was hurt in his voice.

But drawing her close again, Joe tucked her head beneath his chin. "Tell me all about it, Chris Beth."

Settling back into the safe, warm, curled-up position, Chris Beth wondered how she could let the memories or ghosts from the past come between her and this gentle man. One of the things she loved most about him was his *caring*—about her, yes, but about others too. She wanted him to follow the Lord's call. Well, didn't she? Even if it meant taking them away from the roots she had worked so hard to put down here? "Whither thou goest" had been a part of their wedding vows.

She touched his cheek. "It's just that sometimes I think it's all too good to be true—our being here like this—and that maybe it can't last."

"Is *that* all?" Joe hugged her so closely that it was hard to breathe and he could hear his own breath shorten. "I agree with the first but not the second. Just what do you expect to wear out? Not our love, surely?"

"Oh, no!"

"And you don't regret saying 'Yes' to a struggling, country minister's proposal?"

"Oh, Joe, you *know* I don't!"

For one luxurious moment, Chris Beth wound her arms around her husband's neck and snuggled close, wanting to wipe away any hurt she might have caused and longing to share the insecurities she harbored in her heart. But a little whimper from the cradle in the corner reminded her that they were not alone.

Joe grinned. "The look on your face says it would be foolish to ask if you regretted our taking little Mart!"

The very thought brought tears. Joe wiped them away with his thumb. "Then the rest can't matter. Just as long as you don't plan dumping us two and going back to Boston."

"Never, *never*! I'd never leave here—"

There was no further sound from the cradle. The ugly memories were fading more quickly with each return. Maybe the time was right, after all, to mention her concern with their new lives together. *Just mention, that's all I'll do,* she promised herself. *There's such a need for roots. Little Mart deserves that much from us.*

"Joe, you do think we'll be staying—I mean, that there'll be a need for you here?"

Joe looked at her thoughtfully. "I've given it a lot of thought. I know there are needs. And I'm hoping we can hold on till our neighbors can afford us," Joe ended with a smile.

"But if I could teach—"

Marriage is *verboten* in the school's contract. And it wasn't in our plans. I've been thinking that we should take some steps—maybe talk with church boards in other communities—"

"Oh, Joe, no!" The words came before she could stop them.

"I know. I feel the same way, but the ministry requires sacrifices—"

When his words trailed away, Chris Beth knew that Joe wanted with all his heart to remain here. And here they belonged. But she knew too that his first commitment was to the Lord's work, wherever it might lead. The "where" of serving was secondary. *And, for that matter,* she thought with a stir of the familiar bitterness, *so are we—little Mart and I! He's right. The ministry requires sacrifices, maybe too many.*

Immediately she was ashamed of the thought. Joe, she realized, was waiting for her reaction. "We have my salary," she began.

"Chrissy," Joe chided gently. "That ends at the last of the month. And that's not the way we planned it—living on your income."

The gristmill would hardly support the two of them, let

alone Wilson and Vangie and their growing families. Of course, Wilson might sell the botany book he was writing. Or the aging Dr. Dullus might retire on schedule so Wilson could take over his patients. That would help them all indirectly.

Joe interrupted her thoughts. "It's all in the Lord's hands. We are not to worry. It'll all turn out right."

He was right, of course. Hadn't she turned over her worries to the Lord since coming here, and hadn't He done right well with them up till now? Why, counting her blessings would be like trying to count the stars.

Chris Beth was unaware that she smiled until Joe asked, "What's amusing?" and tried to draw her close again.

"A dipper full of stars!" She giggled and pulled away. "Joe! The biscuits will burn."

"I'd settle for that," he smiled, but let her go. "Sunny-side up on the eggs and I'll take care of the baby's needs."

Chris Beth's mind flew busily ahead as she poured fresh honey into the pitcher and set the coffee to heating. She had best prepare herself for the likelihood that one of the churches in the widely scattered neighborhoods would call Joe to deliver a trial sermon. That might mean leaving this beloved cabin, their first home—and how could she part with friends? And what if they called him before school was out? But that was the Lord's business, not hers.

She stopped setting the table when it occurred to her that it was possible they might leave before Vangie gave birth to her baby. She had a doctor for a husband, but a girl needed her mother, or at least an older sister. And in some unreasonable, unexplainable way, she was sure the two of them would need each other more than most sisters. Maybe because the baby was Jonathan Blake's. Somehow that tied them together—bitterly, sadly, but tenderly. Well, the Lord knew about that too.

Joe interrupted her thinking. "We men are hungry! Will you feed us, sweet teacher?"

The baby stirred noisily—another sign of new life around her.

3

Fear of the Unknown

Later that morning Chris Beth decided to pay a call on Vangie. Outwardly she was calm. With little Mart wrapped in a warm blue blanket, she crossed the foot-log spanning the creek which separated her and Joe from Vangie and Wilson. Inwardly, something of the early-morning uneasiness remained even though she had assured Joe she was fine before he and Wilson left to purchase supplies at Solomon's General Store. It was true, really. She would feel better once she and her sister talked.

Vangie was in back of the "Big House," as the four of them distinguished the Wilson place from the Craigs' cabin. She waved and motioned for Chris Beth to join her beneath the peach trees. Chris Beth signaled back that she would wait by the back door, a safe distance from the beehive that her sister had taken on as her private project.

It seemed unsafe to take the baby any closer to the bees than that. And to be honest, she would feel safer to keep her own distance too. Over and over she cautioned Vangie about bee stings. "Bees are like piecrust. They know if you're afraid." And, though singing was more Chris Beth's gift than Vangie's, "I can hum a ring around the bees," she always giggled.

This morning even her humming was off-key. Brahms' *Lullaby* was scarcely recognizable, but the bees didn't seem to mind. Busily they went about the business of gathering pollen from the pink-petaled fruit trees.

"I'm glad you came," Vangie said as she opened the back door and crooked an inviting finger into the big kitchen. "Coffee's still warm, I think."

"And you've baked a coffee cake!"

"Your recipe—but I'm learning!"

Learning lots of things, Chris Beth marveled at her sister's courage and strength. *She's more to be admired than I.* Mama had always overprotected her younger sister, and leaning had become a way of life. Out here where adversity abounded, Vangie had bloomed into a frontier woman almost overnight.

But then Vangie inhaled shakily. "They give me courage—the bees. You know what? This summer I'm going to harvest the honey all by myself—with the baby, of course. I don't want the baby to be plagued by fear like I was. Then," she rambled on, "we can have honey all winter and—"

"Vangie," Chris reprimanded gently when she recognized the sure sign that her sister was avoiding a painful subject.

Vangie stopped, then blurted out, "I—I'm so afraid of childbirth! Oh, I want this baby so much—you understand?"

Oh, Vangie! Her own heart cried out. *Do you really expect me to understand the way you want me to when it's Jonathan's child you are carrying? Can't you see that I'm frightened too?*

Vangie's violet eyes were wide. "You have forgiven me—us—the baby, I mean?"

With that she tumbled into Chris Beth's arms exactly as she used to when it thundered or when her father went into one of his rages. Only Vangie wasn't a little girl anymore. And she was wedging Baby Mart between them.

"There, there," Chris Beth found herself soothing as always. She unpinned little Mart with one hand and tried to support her sister with the other. "Let's talk!" She made her voice purposely brusque. "Now, just what are you afraid of?"

"The unknown. Does that make sense?"

It did. It made more sense than her own fears, which were just the opposite: *known* fears—great green-eyed monsters always standing in the wings, awaiting their cue for reentry, to reenact the tragic moments of her life, to tear down and destroy her new world.

"Chris Beth! What am I going to *do?*" The great, childish china-blue eyes sought her own dark blue ones.

Chris Beth forced a courage she did not feel. "First," she said, hoping to calm her sister, "you are going to hold your nephew. Then you're going to count his pink toes and fingers and enjoy the miracle that God is creating inside *you.* And, while you think on that, I'm going to read our favorite passage. We've been afraid before, you know."

"And you always read the Twenty-third Psalm!"

"Right." Chris Beth reached for the large Bible that she guessed had belonged to Wilson's parents. Somehow it was no surprise that the purple satin ribbon marked the very Scripture that she planned to read.

"The Lord is my shepherd..." she read. "...He restoreth my soul...Yea, though I walk through the valley of the shadow of death, I shall fear no evil...."

At the end of the chapter, Chris Beth stopped. She doubted that Vangie noticed. She was too busy gazing with awe and reverence into the tiny face of the sleeping baby. And softly she hummed the sad-sweet strains of the lullaby she had sung to the bees. Only this time the pitch was perfect.

Life, Chris Beth thought as she crossed the foot-log on her way back to the cabin, *is not a matter of well-executed lesson plans. I can't work out every detail and expect the how, when, and where of it all to unfold on schedule.* Actually, she admitted to herself, she had gone to Vangie to line up forces. Maybe if they both expressed their true feelings about not wanting to leave the settlement... But, even as she thought of such a plot, Chris Beth felt a surge of relief that her sister's needs had changed that. Such action would have been leaving out Joe and Wilson's thinking—and God's guidance. She had overlooked the *why* of it all.

The calm she had pretended before came now, settling on her shoulders like a warm shawl. It was strange how helping another person brought strength to handle her own problems! "Just help me learn to handle them one at a time, Lord, and not without consulting You and Joe...."

4

Guide Us, Lord!

Young Wil ran breathlessly to share the news with Chris Beth instead of going to his own home when he, his Uncle Wilson, and Joe returned from the general store. Although she adored the boy, Chris Beth wished for the sake of the still-new relationship between himself and Vangie that he would not shut her sister out so obviously. He was courteous, Vangie said. Well, that was a start. But Chris Beth knew that more was needed. His first-love crush on her showed signs of developing into the kind of more mature relationship that would leave no permanent scars. As his teacher and wife of his uncle's best friend, and because she and Vangie were sisters, it was essential that there be no jealousies.

"Guess what?" young Wil gasped at the door. Esau's wild barks and the excited honking of the three white geese welcomed him. The boy stopped short, lowering his voice. "Is little Mart asleep?"

Not likely now! Well, then, guess what! Chris Beth couldn't, just as he hoped, so he would have to tell her.

"A *really* big wagon train came just last Thursday, and another one this morning. Then..." He drew a quick breath and rushed on, "...the drivers said a third one's coming over the Applegate Trail—all gonna settle here and—"

Chris Beth was having as much trouble breathing as young Wil. A thrill of excitement filled her. Maybe all their doubts about the future would resolve themselves. Maybe the valley would grow and boom as she, Joe, Wilson, and Vangie had dreamed about around the hearth before the wedding. Waterways opening...railroads coming

23

through...stagecoaches linking California and Oregon from Redding to Portland. That would mean business and new neighbors. Oh, wouldn't it be *wonderful* if—

"You're not listenin'."

"Stop swallowing your g's," Chris Beth said automatically.

"Had to so you'd listen. So *if* you're listening?"

She was. Then there was more, he said. Cattle drivers coming through with herds and herds! Did he know for sure? Well, he had it on "good authority" about the settlers and cattle for sure, and about the other stuff—well, Uncle Wil and Joe *said* it was bound to happen. Wasn't that good enough? Chris Beth nodded happily.

But wait! "Wil, were there children?"

The boy whooped and somersaulted dangerously near the round oak table where supper was laid out. "Hundreds. *Zillions!* There's bound to be more kids than parents, you know."

That figured. Pioneer families were large. But what on earth would she do with even one more student? The one-room school was already overcrowded, and families had pooled every available resource to floor and roof the building. Of course, her contract had only two weeks to go, and most likely the "zillions" of youngsters would be more valuable to their parents at home until next year. Yet there were little Mart and Vangie's baby to think about sometime...but that was a long way ahead. Maybe none of them would be here.

"Miss Chrissy, what about me?" young Wil asked abruptly. "What'll happen to me next year? Will *I* be here, too?"

"I don't know, Wil. I honestly don't know," Chris Beth answered, avoiding his frightened eyes. It had taken her so long to coax the bright young mind into constructive channels. Just remembering brought a set of new concerns.

Outside, the men were unloading grain they had hauled home for grinding. It was hard to tell in the gathering dusk whether their faces showed the concerns that she and young Wil shared.

"We'll just count our pennies in the sugar bowl." She

forced a smile, although the words were closer to the truth than she wanted him to know. "And ask the Lord to help us, of course."

"Right now? I mean the prayer part?"

The question caught her busy mind off guard, but she answered as naturally as possible. "What better time?"

Young Wil hesitated. Chris Beth knew he was struggling with his faith, as well as with his schoolwork and a growing child's changing emotions. To him she was ever the teacher. Whatever concerns she had must be set aside for him, as they had been set aside for Vangie earlier.

"Aw, shucks!" The boy shuffled his worn brogans. Chris Beth noted with tenderness for the motherless child that both his shoelaces were untied. "I don't like praying out loud. Couldn't we just—let's *think* the words. Some I want to keep secret."

"Me, too," she smiled. And the prayer she prayed was simple. "Guide us, Lord," she thought wordlessly, "to accept Your will."

5

Counting Heads—And Days

The sun was just rising on the morning of another school day. Counting this Monday, there were only ten more days to go before school would end for the year. Chris Beth dressed hurriedly, put the coffee on to boil, and checked on little Mart. Although Joe always saw to transporting the little fellow to the Big House, where Vangie kept him until the end of the school day, Chris Beth liked the morning time with him. "Love begins in the cradle," she said repeatedly to Joe. Joe was such a wonderful father...little Mart was such a wonderful baby...and this was such a wonderful country.

All this she thought as she braided her hair and packed a quick lunch. "Truly, Robert Browning was right," she smiled at Joe as he came in from outside. " 'God's in His heaven, all's right with the world....' " And it *was* as her husband hugged her close.

At school, although there were no new heads to count, the children buzzed with excitement. All ran to meet her with the rumor (started by young Wil, she suspected) that soon the school would be "jam-packed" and would need 14 rooms and maybe an upstairs.

"Will they be gittin—gettin'—*getting* here afore school's out?" Harmony Malone wondered.

"Or in time fer the end-o'-school program?" Burtie Beltran asked.

Mercy! She had hardly thought about the program—a "must," the children assured her. But the Basque child had a solution: "I could bring another lamb, like at Christmas."

"Lamb *tongues* ud be better." There was still a high nasal

26

twang to Wong Chu's voice, like a taut bowstring suddenly released. Yet it was amazing how far the Chinese child had come during the school year. But lamb tongues?

"They're flowers, little yellow ones that hide around rocks," young Wil volunteered. "But they grow here, too. Unless maybe we could picnic up at Wong's? I've never been way up there to the railroad camp." He looked at her hopefully.

Chris Beth recalled the shy Oriental father who had won the hearts of the audience by laying his own infant son in the manger in place of the rag doll the night of the Christmas program. She doubted if he would want guests, however. It was best not to push things—just let them happen.

Wong cast his almond-shaped eyes downward. "I'll ask." But before she was able to explain that he need not ask that of his parents, the others were talking.

"We could ride wagons—like when Mr. President come—comed...and there's dogwood...and shootin' stars...and lady's slippers—"

"Orchids," young Wil corrected. Then, turning to Chris Beth, he added, *"Fissipes acaulis,* little purple flowers shaped like a shoe. They're rare."

And so are you, she thought. What a mind!

They were having a wonderful time—children and teacher—when Nate Goldsmith stepped inside the door. There was no reason for the president of the school board to be critical, but Chris Beth doubted if this scene fit his "lick 'em and larn 'em" philosophy. She blushed, hating herself for it.

Her flushed face or the unexpected "company" silenced the children. But, at her signal, they chimed in unison, "Good morning, Mr. Goldsmith!" as she had taught them to greet guests.

Nate Goldsmith answered curtly, adjusted a suspender, and touched his sparse hair nervously. Then he approached Chris Beth.

"Best we speak in private." He motioned to an empty corner.

"Yes, Sir," she answered, wondering what could be so

important. "Boys and girls, quietly go about your work," she pleaded more than ordered. Dutifully she tagged along behind her visitor.

"Warned you I'd be comin'," he said, reminding her of his previous promise.

"You're welcome any time." (But I do wish you'd have warned *when!*)

"Wonder sometimes if you teachers realize jest how important education is." He patted some document in his vest pocket.

"I think we do. We've worked hard."

"Then none o' ye'll have trouble passin' my test."

"Your *what?*" There was only a moment to study the deep lines on his face. Gravity had been his worst enemy, some faraway part of her mind thought, as she noted his nose drooping toward the floor like the beak of a great bird.

"Test! One I conjured up." Mr. Goldsmith pulled a sheet of paper from his pocket—questions for his self-styled "oral examination."

Chris Beth tried to regain her composure. "Wouldn't you like to have me write the questions on the chalkboard?"

"Nope! I'll do it oral. Anyways, you'll be takin' it too." And before she recovered from her surprise, the man was at the front of the room telling the children to prepare for the test "determinin' whether you git promoted or sit here like dummies."

With a roomful of fear-whitened faces looking back at her for support, Chris Beth nodded encouragement and tore a sheet of paper from her rough tablet. And the ridiculous test began.

The hand on her enameled watch crept toward recess, but still Nate Goldsmith's test went on. The first President of the United States. The *now*-president. Your first name. The last letter in the alphabet. The square root of the number of feet in a square mile. How to spell *Constantinople*—by syllables!

"Too bad ye'll not be comin' back," he said to Chris Beth when finally the exhausted children were outside to play. "If'n you passed th' test, it might've meant a five-dollar raise—if crops is good. Need good teachers with all the newcomers. Hear 'bout that?"

Chris Beth nodded mutely. What she and Joe couldn't do with the added five dollars! Or with any job at all, for that matter. But she knew the terms of the contract. "No marryin'." Nate Goldsmith had "warned" her about that, too, she remembered a little bitterly. Still, it was good that he had allowed her to violate the sacred terms long enough to finish the remaining month of the school year.

" 'Marry in haste; repent in leisure,' my old mother used to say."

Fighting for control, she started to protest. "But I—"

He waved away her interruption. "Wait'll I'm finished." He cleared his throat loudly. "I overheerd the talk, y'know, while standin' at the door. We cain't have that."

What had he found so offensive? She tried to remember the talk.

"Talkin' 'bout the business of transportin' children so fur."

"Oh, the end-of-school picnic—"

Again he silenced her with a lifted hand.

"Any picnic'll be hereabouts."

"I hadn't planned—"

"Parents in these parts wouldn't like goin' near them railroad shanties and—" he fumbled for words, "well, mixin' with Chinks."

Something inside Chris Beth exploded. "Mr. Goldsmith, I don't allow the children to speak like that. And, you'll pardon me, Sir," she drew herself up full height, "I'll not allow it of others!"

Immediately she regretted the hasty words. She had made a mistake. Probably the man would not permit her to finish the remaining weeks now. "Lotsa teachers cain't last the year out," he had warned direly when she signed the contract. But she wasn't going to make an apology when she was right. And suddenly she was bold again.

Wiping away the beginning of a tear, she rang the bell sharply. And, before Nate could make a getaway, he was surrounded by bright-eyed children whose coltish play stopped as they lined up to reenter the room. Sensing that something was wrong, they lowered their voices to whispers.

"Boys and girls!" The children straightened. But the warning in her voice was not for them. "Mr. Goldsmith has an announcement!"

She took a near-wicked satisfaction in the man's obvious discomfort.

"We—you—" he said haltingly, "well, there mayn't be a picnic. Leastwise over yonder!"

Young Wil's hand shot up like his cowlick. "You mean to Wong's, Sir?"

Nate tugged at his beard. "Th' same."

"But we *want* to go there—if his folks'll let us. And Miss Chrissy always lets us help decide—"

"Yeah," the other children interrupted, "we wanna go...he's our friend...we wanna go!"

Maybe she should reprimand the children. Well, she wasn't going to. Let him demonstrate the educational "know how" he boasted about.

The chants grew louder. Frustrated, Nate Goldsmith yelled above them, "*I* make the decisions." And with that, the president of the board whirled and stalked out.

The nerve of him! She watched him go, wanting to hit him in the back with the nearest schoolbook.

6

Unbelievable Events

The events of the next two weeks were unbelievable. Chris Beth shared each detail with Vangie, whose "time" was too close at hand for her to risk leaving home. She was hungry to hear of the outside world and hung onto every word.

"It helps me keep my mind occupied and from getting rusty until the baby comes," Vangie kept saying. And invariably she would always ask, "Do you think I should go back to my nursing then—part-time, anyway?"

"You'd be a wonderful help to Wilson. Is he still working on his botany book?"

"When he has time—and when he's not doctoring me. For your sake he's trying to coax the littlest North to hang on until after school closes."

Calling Jonathan's unborn child a "North" touched off the memories again. Of course, Vangie and Wilson *had* hurried up the date of their marriage to make the baby a "true North," they said—

Vangie interrupted her thoughts. "Tell me about today!"

Grateful to get back to the present, Chris Beth shared. And what she shared set both girls to rolling with laughter.

The two of them had decided not to mention Monday's slurring remarks that Nate Goldsmith made about the Chinese family. Joe and Wilson had enough to think about without human relations entering in.

"Well, this morning guess what I found in my trash can?"

Vangie giggled. "A gun with the initials *N.G.* and a notch on the handle."

"I won't be needing a weapon," Chris Beth laughed in

return. "There, wadded into tight balls, were all the answer sheets to that make-believe test he administered!"

On Wednesday, the Goldsmith children gathered around Chris Beth with the news that their pa was coming to school again. And this time he was bringing Ma. It was Ma's first time to visit, they said excitedly. Chris Beth was excited, too, but anxiously so.

The couple arrived in reverse order, with Ma bringing Pa! The little lady looked as defenseless as ever in her dark dress with the white collar and cuffs. But she wore the same determined look that Chris Beth remembered at Turn-Around Inn as she jabbed a prompting elbow into Nate's ribs until he made an "exception to the rule" and allowed Chris Beth to complete the school year—married or not.

"The ole woman has something to say—she wants *me* to say," he said sheepishly.

He hesitated then, but the flash of Olga Goldsmith's eyes warned of a barrage of French-German if he didn't deliver the message in English.

"She thinks—we think—maybe, bein' good Christians and all, we should ought to go to the Chu family's place, after all. Kind of a goodwill gesture, you know. We could surprise 'em."

Above the children's whoops of joy, Chris Beth (trying to keep a straight face) answered, "I think they'd rather know. Wong can help us plan today."

"Us neighbors will arrange some wagons like always—and the dinner and all. Think Brother Joseph can join us?"

Joe? He wouldn't miss this for the world and 10 percent more, she thought. Aloud she said, "I will talk to him."

As it happened, there was no need to plan with Wong. On Thursday he brought his father to school!

Chris Beth was unaware that Mr. Chu waited by the door to be asked inside, until she called the roll and it was sharing time. She began in the usual alphabetical order of names.

But Wong, who was usually very meek, could not wait his turn. "Missie Chrissy, Missie Chrissy!" he burst out. "I 'ave someone!"

It was good to see the boy so eager. Supposing the "some*one*" to mean "some*thing*," Chris Beth was surprised when Wong ran to the door. "My *fath*-er!" he announced happily.

All the other children clapped. Chris Beth felt tears of pride close to the surface. *They've all come so far, so far,* she thought for the thousandth time. *How can I leave them this year?*

Mr. Chu bowed politely to her and then to the class. " 'Scuse please," he said, and reached for the only piece of chalk remaining for the school year. With it he made a series of signs on the chalkboard, which she supposed to be Chinese language symbols. The children were delighted and clapped again.

The man bowed to his son. Wong bowed back. "My father wants me to say you are to come please to the meadow of our home. There the lamb tongues grow."

"Oh, can we—may we—*please!*" Boys and girls alike chorused.

She nodded and Mr. Chu smiled broadly for the first time. "Ancestors will be pleased," he said. Then, tucking his hands inside his kimona-sleeved coat, he padded softly through the door.

● ● ●

Vangie stitched skillfully in and out on the intricate pattern of her latest piece of needlepoint as Chris Beth shared the week's events. Her hands stopped their almost-musical rhythm only when she paused to bite a thread or to laugh.

Chris Beth loved to watch. How like Mama her sister was—so delicately beautiful, so able to shut the whole world out with colored yarn and a piece of canvas! A feeling of homesickness swept over her as she remembered watching the two women together. Swallowing the lump in her throat, she concentrated on the embroidery.

The work was exquisite as always, a rainbow design of flowers, birds, and leaves, as beautifully intermingled as the seasons in the lovely Oregon Country—or the loving hearts of families and friends here. Symbolic and beautiful.

"I wish I had half your talent," she sighed.

Vangie smiled. "Oh, but you do it with people—sort of embroider their lives with love, you know?"

"Oh, Vangie, I will cherish that thought."

"Wilson embroiders with his hands. Just his touch makes people feel better, wouldn't you say?"

The question startled Chris Beth, but Vangie didn't seem to notice. "And Joe makes the world beautiful with words. Finished!" She laid the tapestry aside. "Well, it's been a week of surprises."

Yes, the week had furnished its share of surprises, all right. As Chris Beth carefully catwalked the foot-log back to the cabin on Friday afternoon, she suspected—no, she *knew*—that the next week would afford more. She "foresaw" it.

Some would say it was fantasy, she supposed. Vangie's father would have said it was a "work of the devil." Chris Beth knew it was neither. But just what it was she didn't know—this certain unique power to foresee the future under certain conditions. Always, as now, she first felt a little breathless before a curtain parted in her mind. Today the dizziness passed quickly. She inhaled to still the rapid beating of her heart as spread before her she saw a wide meadow filled with people, their arms linked around her, their song echoing against the hills....

7

The Picnic and Its Revelations

"Circle the wagons!"

The children, not understanding Abe Solomon's remembered call along the Applegate Trail bringing him west from Missouri, giggled and ran excited circles around the wagons, dangerously near the horses' hooves.

"Chil-*dren!*" At the single word from their teacher, the boys and girls quieted down and waited for instructions as to who would be riding in which wagon on the way to Wong Chu's home. Most of them clustered near the wagon carrying the bulging picnic baskets. Chris Beth made a mental note that neither they nor their assorted dogs, including the Norths' Esau and Malones' Wolf, should ride in that one!

"You have a way with children," Mr. Solomon said with shy admiration. "They're gonna miss you. All of us will."

Chris Beth thanked the merchant with a smile, wondering if "we" included his wife and daughter. Mrs. Solomon certainly had "come through" during the winter flood, just as Mrs. Malone had said the older woman always did "in time o' trouble." But there was undisguised regret in her eyes on the day of the double wedding. And her green-eyed daughter Maggie failed to show up at all.

Both women had either Joe or Wilson picked out for Maggie, Mrs. Malone had confided, adding that they would get over the defeat. Well, they'd better. Neither she nor Vangie intended to relinquish her man! But, for all of their sakes, she hoped they would put aside their petty jealousies instead of letting them turn into spite.

Excitement resumed as the children scrambled into their assigned wagons. Chris Beth insisted that O'Higgin and Mrs.

Malone ride in the spring seat of the O'Higgin-Malone wagon. "Joe and I will ride back here with you to guarantee that we get there with the food."

Secretly, for sentimental reasons, she wanted to ride with her feet dangling, as they had ridden to see President Hayes last autumn. Joe was obviously pleased. "Shows our marriage hasn't grown stale," he said with a smile.

"In four weeks? Hardly! We're married for as long as we both shall live. Remember?"

Somehow the words made her uneasy—until Joe took her hand.

As the wagons pulled away from the school, O'Higgin burst into song, his rich, Irish voice rising above the rattle of the wheels over the rutted roads:

> One I loved, two I loved,
> Three I loved, then four—
> Until I met me Mollie-wife,
> And them I loved no more!

"O'Higgin, stop that!" Mrs. Malone said to her husband, but her satisfaction was poorly disguised when the four crowded wagonloads of children joined his throaty song.

The wagons left the school far behind, traveled through the heavy timber, and reached another clearing below which the valley lay. Chris Beth gave a gasp of delight. "It's like a giant opalescent jewel!"

"Worn by a lovely lady as lightly as her laugh," Joe answered.

"We're in a poetic mood—reminds me of our ride in the autumn woods. Oh, Joe, it's good to have an all-season kind of love!"

Her husband squeezed her hand as together they listened to the joyous trills of the nesting meadowlarks and sniffed with appreciation the sweet perfume from the fragile blooms adorning countless budding young orchards. It was good to be alive.

The blended white, cream, and pink blossoms of the fruit orchards—outlined with rims of orange poppies and purple larkspur, and edged by the green forest—was a patchwork of color. "Like one of Mrs. Malone's quilts," Chris Beth said.

O'Higgin overheard. "Yep! Shure and the Lord's good to His children in these parts. Oregon wears heaven's undergarments!"

Chris Beth's eyes feasted on the panorama of color until they fastened on a very large and tumbling building. It was too large to be a house or barn, and she had seen no other fences that tall.

Joe followed her gaze. "The old stockade."

At times like this Chris Beth realized that she had forgotten that she really *was* living on a wild frontier. It was so easy to forget in the comfort of their cabin or when surrounded by friends.

"Are the Indians peaceful now? I mean, are they happy on the reservation?"

"Peaceful, yes. Happy? It's hard to say," Joe said slowly. "We'll pass nearby. You can judge for yourself."

"I never realized the Chinese workers lived so near the Indians. Or how far little Wong rides that donkey—and right by the reservation. Are they on good terms, the Indians and Chinese?"

"At a distance, I'd say. They respect each other, living out the only way of life they know and trusting their own gods—Buddha and the Great Spirit."

"But, Joe, doesn't anybody try to enlighten them?"

"Tell them the story of Jesus? Not since the missionaries. They still talk about the visitor who wore a long black robe and carried a book that 'talked'—probably meant he read to them. Wilson speaks a little of their language and has gathered sketchy information from the young brave who paid you a call at the schoolhouse last year!"

Chris Beth smiled, remembering the day of "Boston Buck's" christening. "Hard telling who was more scared that day—me of an Indian in my classroom or the Indian of Wilson's explosive potion!" She recalled the Indian's horrified look when Wilson fired the warning shot at him.

The young Indian still wore the name Wilson had given him with pride, however. And, although he left no signs, she was sure he frequented the school in curiosity. She was no longer afraid of Boston Buck, but she felt a mixture of concern and fear at passing so near the unseen tribes.

"Do they—uh—like us?"

"Unfortunately, they don't trust us," Joe said regretfully. "You know—the wars, the broken treaties, even the semi-restriction of the reservation. And from what Wilson gathers, the man in the black robe did a lot to twist up their thoughts with his pictures."

"Pictures?"

Joe nodded. "From his book. He used the pictures to reward or to punish. Dealt with the tribes severely, from what Boston Buck remembers of his grandfather's stories."

"But the pictures?"

"When they obeyed him, the man showed them pictures of a beautiful land they call *Siah Close Illahee*. Wilson translates that to mean 'Good Land Far Away.' Said they'd go there when they died."

"And when they didn't obey?"

"Scared them half to death with pictures too dreadful to describe, I guess. A place down below where the wicked go for everlasting punishment. Even looking at the pictures, the way he forced them to, made the Indians *hiyiu cultus seek*—very sick."

"And they never learned about love? Is this story true?"

Joe shifted positions in the wagonbed before answering. "About love, no. But, yes, the brave vouches for the story."

"Where did this missionary finally go?"

"Died here, and supposedly he's buried in the cemetery by the school." Joe studied her face momentarily before continuing. "I think that's where the legend of the strange visitor started—you know, the one who's supposed to haunt the grounds in search—"

Chris Beth felt her face blanch. How well she knew! The legendary apparition was supposed to be searching for his ancestors, Wilson had said. Fortunately, he came only at night when she was gone!

"Could that be why Boston Buck keeps coming back?" she asked. "Hoping to see—"

He sandwiched her hands between his big ones, almost upsetting them both as the wagon jolted suddenly.

"The only one he hopes to see is the lovely Boston lady

with heavy dark braids." He let go of her hands so she could right herself.

"And I aim to keep them! Seriously, Joe, I'm going to find a way to invite him to the Sunday services at Turn-Around Inn."

He took her left hand again and tenderly touched the plain gold band encircling the third finger. "That's why we joined forces here, Chrissy—you and me, Vangie and Wilson—to further God's cause."

Chris Beth realized with regret that they had missed Joe's promised peek of the reservation. Buried so deeply in conversation, she had no time for sight-seeing, but she was glad to have had Joe fill her in on the Indians' background. After all, although it seemed a lifetime, she had been here only since mid-September. There was still a lot more that she needed to know.

Instinctively, even as she and Joe talked, Chris Beth had kept an ear tuned to the voices of the children. She knew they had long since abandoned their wagons and, under the watchful eyes of their parents, were romping alongside the caravan with the dogs. She herself felt cramped from the long ride and was glad when O'Higgin brought the wagon to a sudden halt.

Children surrounded the wagon. "We're here! We're here!"

Wong elbowed his way to her side. "My mother ees finished with the lundree washing." He pointed with pride to a long, sagging line of wet clothing flapping in the breeze. It was easy to recognize Wong's labored printing on the piece of fir wood nailed to one of the line's supporting poles. The letters disregarded all rules of shape, and some were upside down in the child's attempt to print with tar: CHINEZ LUNDRY—FIVE SENS A TUBB!!

Chris Beth felt a warm surge of compassion. "You've done a wonderful job, Wong. Do you help your mother ?"

He nodded proudly. "And Honorable Father help also. No workee seense rails quit."

"Honorable Father" appeared at the door. With a broad smile, he bowed politely and then spoke to his son in his native tongue.

"He show us!" The other children whooped with delight, knowing that Wong meant the wildflowers he had promised.

"Oh, it's good to stretch!" Chris Beth had jumped from the back of the wagon and stood watching as the other adults climbed stiffly from their cramped positions.

"Better put your sun hat on," Joe cautioned. "The April sun can be deceiving, although we'll be lucky if it isn't showering before the day's over."

"Begory! 'Twouldn't be a picnic now, would it, boy, without the rain and the wee ants?" O'Higgin made either sound gleeful.

"We could do without 'em both, but we'll take it in stride," his wife answered as he helped her from the wagon. "Look, Chris Beth," and Mrs. Malone held up a pair of pale blue soakers for her inspection. They were undoubtedly for little Mart. Before she could comment, the incredible woman help up another pair.

"Yellow," she explained, "since there's no way tellin' which the new one'll decide on bein'—boy or girl."

"You mean you knitted instead of relaxing on the way here?" The woman's energy was astounding.

O'Higgin sidled up to stand at his wife's side. "Miss Mollie'll knit at her funeral, she will! 'Tis her way o' findin' peace."

"And most likely, lest you mend your ways in my presence, you'll not be witnessin' it!" Then, turning to Chris Beth, she asked, "Do you want I should stay and help with lunch while you take care of the thunderin' herd yonder?" She tilted her head toward the children, who were eager to be off.

"But there's a lot of work—"

Mrs. Malone waved away the protest. "Nonsense! Jimmy John's sleepin' and there's lots of hands amongst the other women. Some of the men'll want to go along, I'd guess?"

Joe nodded and the older woman continued, "Big boys and other menfolk can hay the horses and catch up easy-like."

And so they were off on an expedition which was to un-cover more than shy wildflowers. For no more had she

turned on her heel than a little rush of breathlessness came.
The curtain of her mind parted to reveal Joe standing in
back of a pulpit, hands upraised. People thronged down the
aisle to meet him. She wanted to join them and stand beside
her husband, where she belonged. But people kept
crowding between them—standing between her and the
joy she should be feeling. What did it all mean?

The curtain snapped shut as she heard the children calling her name. Shaken, Chris Beth hurried up the little hill
to join them.

8

Muslin City

At the top of the little rise, Chris looked to where young Wil and the eldest son of Nate Goldsmith pointed. A narrow path zigzagged up the steep mountain beyond—probably a footpath the Indians had blazed, she supposed—and came to a halt at the broad ledge about halfway up. Above the ledge lay another thick belt of timber.

But the object of the boys' fascination was a cluster of peculiar-looking, gauzelike tents, looking like quickly-spun spiderwebs after a storm. Smoke curled from their midst and formed a sort of halo above them in the morning sun.

"Indians?" Chris Beth was unaware she had whispered the word until Nate Goldsmith himself responded at her elbow.

"Settlers," he said, stroking his beard in concentration. "Sure musta had a devilish time gettin' here over them mountains, 'less they treed the wagons."

Young Wil wondered aloud what "treed" meant.

A drag, Nate explained, meaning a tree hung on behind for "gettin' down faster'n a road'd allow."

Chris Beth shuddered and he nodded. "Dangerous. Lotsa folks claim it'd be more civilized to think 'bout road buildin' instead of school buildin'. Me, I favor education."

The inflection of his voice required a nod. Then Chris Beth turned back to the flimsy tents. "What are they made of?"

"Muslin cloth. Cheap, and so thin that when a body lights up a candle inside, folks can see right through. Keeps insects out, but you'd have t'sleep under a saddle fer privacy!"

"What about fire?" Chris Beth recalled with horror Joe's account of the terrible fire which destroyed the home of his parents, then had snuffed out his mother's life.

Nate turned helpless palms upward. "Not fire season yet, though the rain's stopped early. Them folks'll move or—oh, no, they won't! Will you look at that? See the fellers 'n mules? Cabins soon'll replace Muslin City!"

She looked where Nate pointed and was barely able to distinguish movement in the heavy timber. Men or animals?

"Snakin' poles means they're stayin'. Whadda you know!"

Somewhere from the dense stand of timber came a triumphant call of "Tim-ber-r-r!" followed by a crash that echoed and reechoed against the ledge. Immediately there were shouts and swarms of people everywhere. Then all was quiet where Chris Beth and Nate stood. Too quiet.

"Oh, dear!" She laughed. "We've lost track of our own group." Even Josh Goldsmith and young Wil had left them. "We'd better organize a searching party."

"Plenty help. The other men are comin'. You catch up with Brother Joseph and the kids. Us men better be talkin' over some plans fer the future here in the settlement. We're growin'."

9

Fit for a Prince—Or a Pauper

Head still giddy from the steep climb, arms laden with wildflowers, and heart left in the haze of the redbud grove behind them, Chris Beth descended with the others to join the waiting parents.

"I do believe," she said, catching up with Joe, "that we found the most beautiful spot yet."

Before Joe could respond, young Wil raced back to join them. "Look what we found—Joe and me—for Uncle Wil's book!"

It would have been nice if the boy's timing could have been better. She so wanted to talk with Joe as they strolled the new territory. But young Wil chatted away about the flower he held up. A trillium, and real rare, he said. Did she know that this flower grew in three parts? She did not.

"It does! Grows in three parts—leaves and petals, too— you know, like the Trinity." Chris Beth buried her face in the baby orchids and field lilies, inhaling their fragrance, as young Wil talked.

When finally he ran on ahead, she asked, "Did you see the newcomers, Joe?"

"I did. And I was thinking what a beautiful place for a church back there in the redbud grove. Sort of a central location..."

Joe's voice trailed off and she reached for his hand. If that meant what she hoped, he wanted to stay here as badly as she did. But it would be comforting if he would come right out and say it.

Mollie Malone began to beat the rim of a wagon wheel with an iron spoon just as Chris Beth and Joe approached.

44

Dinner was laid out on snowy cloths spread on the ground under a large, sheltering oak. The other women stood fanning the great platters of fried chicken, homemade breads, and pots of baked beans as if to drive away imagined flies. Their greatest pests were the children. They darted in and out trying to sneak a doughnut or a wedge of devil's food cake without being noticed.

But Mrs. Malone saw. "Not a morsel until the food's blest, you young'uns! Brother Joseph?"

Joe stepped forward. "Bless this bounty, Lord," he said quietly. "And teach us to be more grateful of heart. Let us be sharing neighbors—sharing with every person who crosses our paths this day and every day. And, Lord," he paused, "m-may our every d-decision glorify Your Name. Amen."

The children responded with the Lord's Prayer as planned, with young Wil's voice in lead. Chris Beth was glad that he remembered his cue. Her own mind was less alert. She was too busy trying to interpret the return of her husband's stammer. It was a sure sign that he was under stress. And the part he stumbled over had to do with decisions.

O'Higgin's invitation boomed out: "Step up, folks! Shure and it's a feast we're 'avin, it is. Done by the bonnie ladies and lasses. Fit for a prince, it is."

"Or a pauper," Mrs. Malone said in a near-inaudible voice. Nate Goldsmith called out, "Dig in, kids! It's yore day!" and the children scrambled to heap their plates. Then Chris Beth's glance caught the older woman's eye and followed it.

There, at the top of the little knoll leading toward the ledge, stood a long line of dirty, ragged children. Even at a distance, their sad, too-large eyes said starvation. With gaping mouths, they stared at the food in a hungry—almost animalish—way.

"Immigrant children. And starvin' to death, poor babies," Mrs. Malone whispered to Chris Beth. "Applegate Trail folks, for sure."

Chris Beth felt her scalp prickle. She had heard the horror-and-sorrow stories of that route into Oregon. Who hadn't? But she had never seen what it did to the children. All her appetite left her.

"What will we do?" She questioned desperately, unaware that she had spoken aloud.

O'Higgin, who spotted the children then, waited for no instructions. "Come here, ye wee ones!" he called lustily and waved a drumstick in invitation.

Frightened, the children turned to leave. Young Wil saw them and held out a ball made of discarded twine. "Catch!" he ordered, tossing the ball in the air. It fell short of where the children stood, but one of them ventured forward and shyly picked it up.

"Throw it back and let's get a game going. But come on down. We've all got to eat first. Teacher's rule!"

Chris Beth could have burst with pride in the boy. She felt a tear trickle down her cheek and was dimly aware that Joe wiped it away with his thumb as the children advanced.

It took some gentle urging from Mrs. Malone for the children to accept food. But once the tallest of the group, a gaunt, redhaired boy, reached for a slice of thickly buttered bread, the others followed. "Eatin' like a bunch o' coon hounds," Nate said in quiet satisfaction.

As the children finished second helpings, Chris Beth saw something that made her heart turn over with pity. The boy who had accepted the bread dropped to his knees, looked around fearfully, and snatched as much of the bread as his two sunburned hands could hold. Warily he stuffed it into the pocket of his ragged pants.

Mrs. Solomon saw, too. "Let's not be frightenin' 'em away now. The Lord knows their needs and He's found a way to supply 'em."

"You're so right, Bertie," Mrs. Malone agreed. "And we all of us know this food would be spoilin' on us before we reached home."

Yes, they all knew. So who would take the leftovers to the newest neighbors? Men know how to talk to men, the men said. But us women know how to talk to women. And everybody had witnessed that children know best how to talk to children. So best they *all* go. Could just finish the picnic up there.

Back up the little knoll they went. Then, with directions

from the now-talkative children, it was on up to the ledge and the muslin tents. Chris Beth wondered, as they trudged upward, what sort of reception they would receive. She saw that the games so carefully planned, the program so carefully rehearsed, and the visiting which the women cherished so much were now forgotten by all. But something infinitely more important was taking place.

"You're wearing the look that's so becoming," Joe said, suddenly catching up with Chris Beth and matching his steps with hers. "Happy?"

"Very!" But there was no time to say more. "Cap'n Jack," as the man introduced himself, extended a callus hand in welcome. "I'm sort of navigator and wagon master here. And this is my recent wife. Lost my other one, rest her soul, on the trail. Never thought any one of us would make it."

The pale, sad-faced young woman, jostling a crying baby on her hip, came forward. Suddenly the men, women, and children divided into their respective groups. "The young'uns have been fed," Mrs. Malone explained to Captain Jack's wife. "Some of the older folks as well—men, mostly. But us womenfolk—well, we like t'talk and eat without bein' interrupted." Without further ado, she set about unpacking the picnic baskets again.

Chris Beth moved among the women, introducing herself. "I'm Mrs. Craig, wife of the handsome minister over there." Invariably the words coaxed smiles from mouths that looked unaccustomed to smiling. And small wonder, she thought, as she listened to the pitiful accounts of the wagon train's three-month tortuous journey from the Mississippi Valley and their reasons for coming West.

"We all had the ague, just shook with it," the nervous and rapid-talking Mrs. Cliborn explained. "Then there was hot summers and bitter winters. Then them cockleburs was taking over farmground. Me and my man, we figured 'twas as good dyin' on the trail as shakin' to death with ague—or starvin'. 'Course, little did we know!"

Well, they found out, she said. And the others joined in— the shy, sandy-haired Mrs. Emory; Mrs. Westmoreland, the capable lady who reminded Chris Beth of Mrs. Malone; and all the others, none of whom seemed to have much in common except for the agonies suffered along the Applegate Trail and the desire for a better life here in the Oregon Country.

Well, there was one thing more—their concern for their men. Even as the women talked, they kept excusing themselves one by one to reload plates of food for their husbands, who stood apart from the women, often scraping their plates loudly in signal for refills.

Chris Beth was relieved to see that the food was holding out. She wanted so much to help these people. She wanted—and needed, too—to hear their stories as well. It made her realize that her own trip to Oregon by stagecoach had been easy compared to what the Mississippi travelers had suffered. "I remember most the storms, women and children hid under mattresses, men struck down by lightnin', and all our belongin's blowed away.... Me, I recall most the floods, washin' away our last cow, then the awful mire up to the axles afterward.... Not much hurt me like havin' to discard Mama's walnut bureau—throwin' it down the mountain, hearin' it splinter below...but nothin'—*nothin'* (the women covered their faces then) compared to the other..."

"The other?" Chris Beth asked of the chatty Mrs. Cliborn.

"The scalpin's," she whispered. Chris Beth felt herself choke on the single bite of food she had taken, as the woman went on. "Indians, you know, painted and screamin'—killed whites by the hundreds—had to bury folks we loved in one grave, the few of us," she nodded toward the group around them, "left out of the eight hundred."

"Eight hundred!" Why, there were fewer than a hundred here now.

"And lost near that number, countin' the ones born on the way." Chris Beth was thankful when the woman changed to a lighter topic. "And what I *missed* most was soap! We're washrag people where I come from."

Mrs. Emory spoke up shyly. "What I missed was fresh fruit—well, any food at all after a while. But at first it was fruit I craved, expecting the baby."

Mrs. Cliborn interrupted. "And then to cap the climax, you shoulda seen what happened along the river at Fort

Vancouver. My pore little Lecretia here was standin' lookin' at a boatload o' sailors unloadin' cargo. One yelled, 'Hey, little lady, have uh apple!' She tried and tried to catch 'em with her skirt, but they was laughing at her petticoat 'n all till she dropped 'em. Just had to stand and see 'em float down the Columbia whilst they laughed. But tell me now, are these apple dumplin's?"

"Ladies, we must be goin'," Abe Solomon said, looking at his pocket watch.

There were hasty good-byes, fervent thank yous, and warm invitations for the callers to return. "And soon!" Chris Beth promised as she squeezed back the tears. The thread-bare garments, the pitifully inadequate "tents," the hunger—all of it had wrenched her heart.

"Sure hope they have the stayin' power," Mrs. Malone said as she and Chris Beth hurried back down the knoll to where the men were hitching up the teams. "We've got a powerful job ahead helpin'."

They were down the hill by then, and O'Higgin heard his wife's last words. "But crops be the best yet. We're able! Where's me plaidie, Mollie Love?"

Mrs. Malone handed her husband his woolen cape and he spread it on the wagon bed for Jimmy John. As the caravan was about to pull away, there came a call of, "Welcom 'gin. Vellee good!" in Mr. Chu's broken English. It was Nate who responded.

"Sure, Brother! See you for Sunday services at the brush arbor, weather permittin'. Just glad us folks thought of comin' here fer the day's outin'!"

Chris Beth sat down gratefully on the back end of the O'Higgin-Malone wagon. It was good to relax beside Joe and dangle her feet after the long, strange day. "Joe," she said, "there were some startling revelations today, weren't there?"

Joe appeared to consider, then said, "Most revealing was hearing you introduce yourself. You could have called yourself the teacher. Instead, you said you were my wife. I liked that."

10

Singin' Against the Dark

Joe reached for Chris Beth's hand as O'Higgin turned the wagon toward home. She felt a great rush of love mingled with excitement. "I'm a silly goose," she mused half-aloud. "Being away from little Mart this long seems forever!"

"Sauce for the goose is sauce for the gander," he whispered in her ear, and together they giggled at his use of Mrs. Malone's favorite words of weapon to make her point with O'Higgin.

"Do you know, Joe, that I know so little of the baby's background—I mean, I hardly met his poor parents, the Martins before they died during the flood. What were they like?"

"I didn't know them well either—just who they were. They were very young, and she was well-educated but homesick for Missouri. No sickness like it, you know."

How well she knew!

"Never saw her wear anything but black with white collar and cuffs. Very shy, too. All traces of their background washed away in the flood—but does it matter?"

"No," she answered slowly, "except for little Mart's sake, when the time comes."

He squeezed her hand hard. "We'll manage. And speaking of time, isn't Vangie's baby overdue?"

Chris Beth had been worrying about that, although Wilson had told her repeatedly that it was not unusual for the first baby to be late. But poor little Vangie was miserable—and scared.

Her thoughts were broken suddenly by a distant wail of fiddles. "Swing your partners right and low!" a male voice called, and the clapping of what sounded like a thousand hands picked up the rhythm.

"The newcomers," Mrs. Malone called over her shoulder, "singin' against the dark." The poignant notes faded away.

As the lowering sun turned the snow on the mountain peaks from rose to mauve, Chris Beth was grateful for the long twilights of the Oregon Country. There was a lot she wanted to talk about and sort out in her mind.

"The people back there—will they manage?" she asked Joe.

"With our help," he answered.

"But," she hesitated, "Joe, we have so little—"

"We have everything, everything that c-counts."

Except a job, or an income, or maybe even a future here, Joe's slight stammer said plainly.

Chris Beth longed to share her own insecurities. But how could she explain the phenomena which kept transporting her mind to places and situations yet to be experienced? It was not that Joe would laugh at her, but what was there to tell? Her head said there was a reasonable explanation, but her heart said something else. The Lord was speaking to her—maybe sometimes *through* her—but until she knew *what* He was saying, the visions must be put away in some corner of her heart like she had stored the brooch at the bottom of the camphor-wood chest.

Aloud, she shared only the happy part of the repeated vision. "Everything that counts, indeed! We're surrounded by people we love and who love us in return."

The sky turned navy blue. The unmistakable bass hoots of a night owl said the wagons were nearing the forest. Sensing danger, the gray squirrels scampered up and down the fir boughs so haphazardly that they tumbled against each other in their efforts to escape the claws of the forest monarch. Blue jays sounded a raucous alarm from the top-most branches. Then all was silent— until the crickets and katydids tuned up their own fiddles as if they too were singing against the dark. Chris Beth felt the same wonder and awe she had felt on first coming into this wild, new land where neighbors needed one another just as the forest creatures did.

"Did you happen to meet a Mrs. Robbins among the newcomers?"

Chris Beth wondered if Joe had asked her more than once. She had been so lost in thought that words could have gone unnoticed. "No," she responded tentatively. "Not that I remember, anyway."

"You'd remember. Her husband says she knew you, or knew *of* you. Seems your mother had spoken of your being here—you or Vangie. He asked of you both by name."

Chris Beth's blood ran cold. "By *name*?" She whispered the word through tight lips. "First or last?"

"Both. He seemed to know you were half sisters. You'll probably enjoy news from home." His voice was suddenly concerned. "Are you cold?"

Not really. Not in the way Joe meant. But she snuggled close for comfort. *Vangie—poor little Vangie*—who had used her maiden name as a shield against people's knowing her child was illegitimate.

11

True North

It was lighter as the wagon pulled out of the woods and onto the main road. "We'll walk from here," Joe offered at the crossroads. Young Wil, eager to share his rare trillium find with Wilson, raced toward home before waiting for Chris Beth and Joe.

"Shure and ye'll be spoonin' before the wagon's over the wee hill," O'Higgin said jovially as he drew the team to a stop. "So'll me and me Mollie-love, most likely."

"Behave yourself, O'Higgin!" Mrs. Malone lifted a hand to tuck a stray lock of graying hair into her tight bun, and her Irish husband dodged the pretended blow with a roguish roll of his eyes.

"Been a wonderful day, thanks to Nate," she said in mock sincerity. "Did you ever see the beat of how that man takes credit for every miracle in the settlement?"

The families shared an understanding laugh; then, after sleepy good-byes from the Malone children, the wagon moved toward their home at Turn-Around Inn.

"Let me know when Vangie's confinement comes. I"ll be helpin', you know!" Miss Mollie's voice called.

"One I loved; two I loved..."

O'Higgin's mellow voice rose, then faded as the wagon topped the hill and disappeared. Hand in hand, Chris Beth and Joe turned home. Yes, it had been a wonderful day, filled with surprises and opening the gates for more, but Chris Beth felt an urgent need to be back with Vangie and little Mart. Maybe Joe noticed, for his step quickened. She matched his long strides, hoping that the feeling of apprehension was only her imagination.

"Vangie," Joe spoke suddenly. "Back there when I mentioned Mrs. Robbins—"

But whatever he had been about to say went unsaid. The air around them split by Esau's excited barking and the frightened screams of young Wil.

"Hurry! Hurry! Vangie—the baby—little Mart—"

Chris Beth's heart hammered so heavily against her ribs that it was hard to run. In her terror she broke away from Joe and cut through a thicket of heavy brush laced with wild blackberry vines. The briars tore at her flesh, but she felt no pain.

At first Chris Beth was sure something had happenend to little Mart. He was screaming lustily, which both frightened and comforted her. Then, before she could unfasten the latch of the Big House's front door, she knew it was Vangie. Her agonized moans were coming from the front bedroom. Later she was unable to remember how she managed to get inside or when she became aware that little Mart was lying safely in an ancient cradle alongside the bed where her sister lay writhing in pain. Wilson stood over her.

"Chris Beth! Hot water! Clean sheets in the bureau!"

But Chris Beth could only stand frozen in terror at the sight of Vangie's blanched face, her body doubled grotesquely and her tiny fists clenched against the convulsive contraction.

"Chris Beth!" Wilson's voice carried a command, lost on Chris Beth.

"We'll have to have Mrs. Malone—"

"There isn't time! *You'll* have to help."

"Me?" Her voice sounded far away even in her own ears. "But I don't know—I've never seen—"

Wilson ignored her completely. He was suddenly a man she had never known before. All doctor. And she—not Vangie—was nurse.

Bring water. Mop brow. Hand him the damp cloth. Hold Vangie down until the contraction was over. Move. Hurry. Don't think. Don't feel. Just work. And hurry. And *pray*!

Yes, pray, for things were not going right. Even in her

inexperience, Chris Beth knew. Maybe they were losing the battle.

"Wilson," she whispered once, "Wilson, is she going to make it?"

That's when he had said, "You know how to pray, don't you?"

Dimly she was aware that little Mart had quieted down. Young Wil and Joe were talking in subdued tones. And there was the unmistakable aroma of coffee. That should have been bracing. But instead it made her sick. "Wilson," she gasped.

Seeing her white face, Wilson—without change of expression—said brusquely, "Go get rid of it and get back here with me!"

Outside, Chris Beth allowed herself only a minute to be sick before hurrying back to the nightmare. Faint as she was, it never occurred to her to leave Vangie's side. At least, although queasy, she felt a certain pride in the fact that she was seeing it through. Vangie needed her—always had, but now as never before.

And even as the thought came to her, Vangie spoke her name.

"Chris Beth—"

Vangie's voice was nearly inaudible. Chris Beth leaned close to hear the faint words.

"If—If I don't make it—you'll love the baby?"

"Don't talk like that!" Tears streamed down her face so fast she was unable to wipe them away with the back of her hand.

"Chris Beth—you'll raise the baby as a true North—"

The question was so startling she was unable to answer. It had never occurred to her that she might have to raise Jonathan's child!

"Promise—" The childish voice was weaker.

"I promise, Darling, I promise—"

Vangie dozed fitfully. "Wouldn't you like coffee, Wilson?" Chris Beth whispered across the sheet shielding Vangie's quivering form. Maybe if she could get away—even a minute—things would come into focus. But Wilson was shaking his head.

"No, don't leave. I don't like the way things are going.

The baby's too small. Heartbeat's faint. In a wrong position—" Vangie stirred and he leaned over her, motioning Chris Beth to move closer.

"She's pale, Wilson," she whispered, then said desperately, "Oh, Wilson, is she going to make it?"

Wilson shot her a hard look. Maybe it was meant to silence her, but the look revealed more to Chris Beth. It told her that Wilson was scared too.

"Of *course* she'll make it!" He ground the words out through clenched teeth. Then, as if talking to himself, Wilson continued in a hoarse whisper, "She has to, Lord. She *has* to! But she should have delivered before now—she's weakening and the delay's doing the baby no good—Oh, God!"

There was a cry of anguish from the bed. Vangie, almost wild in her pain, rolled from side to side and would have fallen from the bed had Wilson and Chris Beth not restrained her.

"Hold her down!" Wilson's tone was sharp. "And wipe her face."

Chris obeyed automatically. Wilson watched, biting his lip in concentration. Then, in a somewhat softer voice, he said, "Brace yourself, Chrissy. It's going to take all we have within us to save Vangie and the baby—maybe either of them."

"What are you going to do?" she whispered desperately as again she mopped Vangie's ashen forehead. "Wilson! Her lips are blue! What can we do?" She felt cold sweat form on her own face.

"I have to take the baby. It's a risk and you have to help me or we'll lose them both. Do you hear?"

She heard, but she didn't believe. It couldn't be. If her little sister was going to be taken from her, she couldn't witness it. "I can't, I—"

But her words were drowned by Vangie's scream. The scene took on a feel of unreality. She gathered her sister close and whispered words of comfort. She herself was in the lap of a great pain. Then she felt nothing at all as she handed items to Wilson on command and repeated after him the words he told her, "Push...relax...once more..."

Somewhere a clock chimed midnight, then one o'clock...

two...three.... "She's too exhausted to help," Chris Beth whispered. "She's not responding to me, Wilson." She wondered then if the still form was moving up and down with breath. In a near-primitive effort to preserve life, Chris Beth urged, "Push...relax...push, Vangie!"

As the clock struck five, Wilson spoke for the first time in hours. "You'll have to come here. The baby's head is turned wrong. *Hurry*! It's choking!"

Choking. The baby was choking. Vangie's baby! It no longer mattered who the father was. Nothing mattered except saving the little life. And the mother's. *Nothing* else mattered. Not her own feeling. *Nothing at all.*

Through a white haze she saw Vangie's even-whiter face. "Hang on, Chrissy," Wilson whispered. "You're doing fine. Hang on. We need you—"

Vaguely Chris Beth was aware that Vangie's screams had stopped. Through the haze around her, she tried to read Wilson's exhausted face. "What happened?" she gasped. "Did she—did we—?"

But Wilson dropped on his knees beside the still form amid the sweat-soaked sheets. He was whispering little words of endearment. Panic rose to her own throat. And then she saw the tiny bundle that Wilson was laying beside her sleeping sister. Alive! Both of them...

Suddenly a wild laugh rose to her lips. "You mean—you mean we made it? We—you and I—we delivered a baby?"

"Come and see," Wilson said without looking up. "Just come and take a peek at your little niece."

Niece! She had a niece. Vangie had delivered her "true North."

With a deep sense of emotion—almost as if she had been God's helper—Chris Beth looked at the tiny piece of humanity. "Did she have a name picked out?" she asked foolishly.

"Trumary," he whispered, getting up from his knees. "True North! And *now* we'll have that coffee! My wife and daughter must rest."

12

Heartbeats of Heaven

Chris Beth gasped with delight at the first glimpse of her new niece. She noted with relief that every infant feature was Vangie's. *And Vangie's alone!* The delicate skin...the little tuft of golden hair already threatening to curl...even the Cupid's-bow mouth that made her look like the china doll Mama used to keep on the mantle. Thinking of Mama made her sad. Mama should know about her granddaughter.

But Vangie's face had blanced at the suggestion. "Oh, no! Chrissy—*promise!*"

"No promise is necessary, Darling," Chris Beth assured her sister. Both of them knew that getting mail to their mother was virtually impossible now that the one remaining servant had been dismissed. "We both know that your father—my stepfather— wouldn't let us be in touch. And certainly not about the baby."

"I hate him. I *hate* him!"

'Vangie, you mustn't. We have to forget." Chris Beth pulled Vangie near in an effort to soothe her.

Vangie drew away. "But to throw me out, isolate me from our mother, all for one mistake—and the *baby* is not a mistake! She's the greatest thing God ever created!"

"Except for little Mart," Chris Beth agreed, and was relieved to see Vangie smile. She knew, however, that all ties with home were severed, barring a different kind of miracle.

"Dear little heartbeats of heaven," Mrs. Malone declared of the sleeping babies when she came calling as quickly as corn planting and setting out the tomato plants would allow.

58

"Livin' proof the Creator intended life in this world should go on!"

And life went on in the settlement, too. O'Higgin's "Bossie" came home with a new calf, so the girls were able to have fresh milk for the little ones. Wild strawberries stained the hills and neighbor children weeded the corn rows fast so they could slip up the ridge, out of the sight of slower-moving adults, and fill pails—after they filled themselves. The pails of wild fruit they brought to Vangie and Chris Beth "fer eatin' with Jersey cream." Birds stopped quarreling and chose mates. No hoped-for rain was in sight, but the water table was high from the heavy rain storms of the winter, keeping the valley lush and green.

Chris Beth took Mrs. Malone's advice and "stored against the winter," making use of her jelly-making skills learned from "Cook" in her childhood and learning how to sun-dry early fruit. Vangie harvested the honey from her well-tended hives and sewed with inspiration. Easter was late, and what better time to show off both new babies?

"Wasn't it sweet of Mrs. Malone to include scraps in the layette she gave me for a wedding gift?" Vangie's eyes held a Christmas-glow. "So right for our 'heartbeats of heaven'!"

13

Easter at the Arbor

On Good Friday Wilson surprised Vangie, Chris Beth, and Joe by bringing a secondhand carriage home when he returned from his weekly delivery of ground wheat and corn. "Abe probably skinned my teeth out," he grinned in telling how Mr. Solomon had bargained to get the two-wheeled cart that Wilson had used for transportation.

While Vangie and Chris Beth looked excitedly at the new vehicle, Wilson and Joe talked of the progress around the general store. Although excited over the two leather-covered seats and the fancy fringe around the top, Chris Beth listened to Vangie with only one ear and was glad when young Wil, equally excited, came to talk with Vangie. Her other ear had been tuned in on the men's talk, and she wanted to hear more.

Some of the conversation was good—the part about the progress. The rest of their talk frightened her.

"The Muslin City people were just a handful of the newcomers," Wilson was saying. "The Solomons say the store's surrounded with them. And the store was a madhouse. Miners. Ranchers. Farmers. Few businessmen."

Joe listened intently. When he spoke, she was sure he lowered his voice.

"Any talk of a doctor?"

Wilson laughed easily. "Nope! No preachers, either. Or, for that matter, teachers or nurses. They're hard to come by—or keep."

Chris Beth was unable to hear Joe's reply, but Wilson broke in to say, "I wouldn't worry too much. They're going to have to have us eventually, and, like O'Higgin says,

60

crops never looked so good. And, Joe," Wilson said, as he unhitched Dobbin and the one-eyed horse named Battle he had traded some pelts for, "the rails are coming. Half the men in the store have been hired already!"

"That means we can ship our goods and get people in and out instead of waiting for the stage."

"But, wait, I haven't told you what the other half was hired for!"

"You mean—"

"What I'm meaning is that the waterways are going to open for sure. But let's wait and share the rest with the girls."

The two men moved away, but not before other fragments of the conversation reached Chris Beth. Wilson had seen "Doc," and, sure enough, he was going to stop doctoring.

"But that might mean we'd have to move into town—and *town* it'll be all right. Did I tell you that an assayer has up a sign? Oh, the Solomons plan a hotel...progress brings the other, too...yeah, dance hall...reports of dance hall women...hard to keep the seamy side of society out."

Joe voiced concern about money, and Wilson gave a characteristic shrug. There'd be need for doctors and preachers with all the new element coming. Joe smiled and Chris Beth did too, until she distinctly heard Wilson mention the name *Robbins*. Then her heart gave an extra beat. Wasn't that the name of the woman who knew Vangie as Mary Evangeline *Stein*? If she let the name drop around the store, it would be all over town. Then everybody would know that Vangie had not been a young widow at all— just a "wayward girl"—and that her child had been on the way, unblessed by marriage, when the frightened 17-year-old girl came to the settlement to hide in disgrace.

How horrible! *I must talk it over with Joe,* Chris Beth thought. *Now is the time—maybe at supper tonight.* Meantime, she mustn't worry.

But, try as she would, it was impossible to dismiss the fears. Memories of "poor little Becky Lee" haunted her memory—the frail little outcast who stood aloof, watching as the other children played. "You can't play with *her*! She's a ____!" They dropped their voices then—dropped them so low that Chris Beth and Vangie were never able to distinguish the word.

"What does it mean, Mama?" Chris Beth, being older, was always the speaker. And Mama would shut out the question with slender, blue-veined hands.

"Poor little Becky Lee," she would moan. Then she would say something mysterious like, "It means her mother's a bad woman. Poor little Becky Lee. But you must not even *talk* about such things or you will be bad, too." Then she and Vangie would pray that never, ever would they be bad. Bad like poor little Becky Lee's mother....

At supper, when they were alone at the cabin, Joe had some news of his own. "I'll be preaching Sunday," he said without preliminaries.

"You'll *what?*"

Joe smiled at her surprise. "I did tell you I was a preacher?"

"Stop teasing, Joe. When—how—why didn't you tell me!"

Joe looked more serious. "I take it you're pleased, but," he cautioned, "don't attach too much to it. I offered at the picnic when I heard Jonas' rheumatism had worsened. No longer able to ride the circuit."

"But doesn't this say the people want you, if they ask you?"

"It does. What it *doesn't* say is that they want me permanently—or that they can pay—"

" 'Less'n crops are good and folks kin meet their taxes,' " she mimicked Nate's admonitions when she signed the contract to teach.

"Now *you* be serious." Joe captured her hand and held it as she was about to spoon gravy over his second slice of venison roast. "I just don't want you planning too much. You might as well know I'll be preaching at Willow Grove—just filling in—the next Sunday after Easter."

Willow Grove was miles away. Yes, and they would want to meet his wife. *But little Mart?* No problem—Vangie would take him in. *But what did Joe want to do? Where was his calling?* These questions Chris Beth did not ask. She knew the answers already. Joe would know them Sunday.

But on Sunday he did not know, she thought, as the two

families rode toward the brush arbor for outdoor services. At least, the answers hadn't come yet. Joe was even quieter than usual. But who wouldn't be when confronted with preaching a first sermon, even to friends? A little chill ran down her own spine at the very thought. *How silly*, she thought, and concentrated on the beauty of the morning.

"I'd know it was Easter even if nobody told me!" Vangie said above the chuckle of the new buggy wheels.

"True," Chris Beth answered, adjusting the brim of her wide hat to shield little Mart's face. The snow was gone from their side of the mountain, except for the fretted lace along the top, and in its place a million pink and white azaleas in trumphant bloom came down the slopes to meet the valley. Somewhere a robin called, plaintively at first; then, as if joy overcame all doubt, he poured out his song of elation. Something inside Chris Beth responded. It was Easter—the Lord's day of triumph!

Never had there been such a day. And never had there been such a sermon. *Nobody* could've reached 'em all like that, the valley folk said.

'Em all referred to the great number of totally unexpected worshipers who were congregated already when the buggy pulled in from the main road—a crowd which almost doubled before the singing was finished. And small wonder, Chris Beth thought with a smile. O'Higgin was at his best at leading the singing. His red hair seemed to pause for breath only whenever members of the congregation called out a request. Then, in the midst of "Glory to His Name," the man got himself carried away and went into something akin to an Irish jig. "Oh, the devil's mad and I am glad!" he called out lustily. "Sing on, brothers and sisters—second verse!"

Chris Beth, having forgotten all misgivings, leaned back and joined the group. And, like the robin, she felt her own doubts dissipate and her song turn to pure joy. "Watch it, or you'll be dancing around with O'Higgin," Vangie whispered, then, in astonishment, put a finger to her own lips. Both girls realized it was the first time either of them had whispered in church.

When Joe rose to "take the pulpit," as Nate announced he would do, the demon of misgiving returned to snuff out

Chris Beth's earlier exultation. It was as if, suddenly, she and Joe were transported back to last night's supper table.

"Maybe I'm not r-ready," Joe had said haltingly.

"Stop doubting yourself, Darling," she had begged. "You know you'll do a great job."

But Joe had ended their talk with a stammer which made her apprehensive. "I—I *don't* know—that's the problem. And a f-first sermon means so much. To me. And to *them*. D-don't you know it'll leave a lasting i-impression?"

Yes, she did. She knew last night. And she knew now. Doing the job well today was important to Joe because the ministry was his life. And today he was on trial. But Chris Beth could only think of what his success today meant to her—staying. Unconsciously she folded her hands and closed her eyes in unspoken prayer.

She caught her breath when Joe murmured a thank you to Mr. Goldsmith. *If I keep my eyes closed, maybe the problem will go away,* Chris Beth thought foolishly. And then Joe was speaking!

Her eyes flew open and focused anxiously on his face. He looked calm, but his words said he was not. "Th-thank you, too, O'Higgin. The singing was w-wonderful."

Anxiously Chris Beth looked around her. The faces of the audience told her nothing. Apparently their ears had failed to pick up the telltale stammer. Then, when her eyes met her husband's, she realized that he was looking at her for strength. She forced a little smile. Then, miraculoulsy, Joe was in control. She saw it in his eyes. "Thank you, Lord," she whispered reverently. "He made it over the first hurdle. Now *You* take over from here!"

"God bless you all!" Then quietly, almost gently, Joe greeted the audience by name. The transition from the workout in song that O'Higgin had given the group was perfect. Pleased to be recognized, each family stood when he spoke out: "And good morning to the Smiths—the Beltrans—and the Solomons."

"Did you take notice how long Maggie was in standin'?" Mrs. Malone was to ask later. Yes, she noticed. And she noticed, also, that until the girl stood, her green eyes were fixed on Vangie. She knows, Chris Beth thought in the split-second time that her own eyes intercepted the revealing glance.

But there was not time to give the matter further thought. Joe had asked each "old-timer" (and with a thrill of joy she realized that included her and Vangie) to look about them, center out the face of at least one newcomer, and smile. She felt tears close to the surface as her glance caught sight of the faces of people in the Muslin City settlement they had met on the last day of school. Then the tears were out of control when she saw Wong—and, miracle of miracles— Mr. Chu and behind him the tiny figure of his wife.

Yes sireee! It was a wonderful service, all right. Conducted just right for new folks. Brother Joe was a called preacher, fer sure—not any fancy words or "scary stuff," just "Bible talk."

When the crowds pushed in around Joe to shake his hand, Chris Beth felt such a thrill of joy that she was sure her heart would burst. Surely, *surely* nothing could go wrong now. She wanted to be beside him to tell him what she was thinking, but the crowds were moving ahead...and this was their time with him; she would wait.

Waiting gave an opportunity to remember fragments of Joe's beautiful sermon. "Easter is a time of hope and faith," he had said. "The farmer, forgetting last year's small harvest, tills the soil and seeds it again, knowing the harvest will come. And the Christian, forgetting the trials and losses of last year, has the same reassurance. As the seed must die to be born again, so must man's body. But Easter is our hope. Easter is God's promise of life after death through the resurrection. We wilt; we wither; we become a part of the earth. But the Lord is frugal, like the farmer. Nothing in His heavenly kingdom is wasted, especially the soul of mankind. So rejoice and be glad."

With that, the crowd drowned out Joe's words with shouts of joy. During his short benediciton, Chris Beth breathed a prayer of her own: "It was a beautiful sermon, Lord, and he didn't even stutter!"

The crowd at last drifted from beneath the arbor. The newcomers would have turned back to the ledge, but the settlers would have no part of such. Why, sakes alive, there was twice more'n was needed—want all them cakes and pies to go beggin'?

"Did you ever see so much growth at Eastertime?" Mrs. Malone marveled. "Babies, new folks, and all the greenin'." Then, raising her voice, "Come see my grandchildren!" she invited.

Vangie smoothed imagined wrinkles from her baby's long white dress and, with a rapturous look, held her out for all to see. "And I'm just as bad," she smiled to herself, "holding little Mart out like an offering." Well, wasn't he an offering—a special offering to the Lord? With that thought a general sense of well-being crept over her.

Why, then, was there a catch in her throat and a peculiar sense of unreality? The crowds she had envisioned had materialized. And while it was true that she had been unable to make her way to stand beside Joe, they were among friends. For today she would rejoice and be glad.

14

Stay...Stay...Stay!

May brought the rhododendrons out in a scarlet blaze of glory. Usually noted for their good sense, old-timers claimed, the tree-tall evergreens bloomed in a breathtaking explosion of color instead of testing a few secluded spots. April showers had been sparse, and these flowering plants found May's warm breath to their liking. "Too docile," farmers complained, scratching their heads. "May weather's not shapin' up proper-like."

Chris Beth understood their concern. First there were winter's torrential rains, and now a near-drought meant lush growth. It was good for the gardens and early hay-cuttings, but bad for the forests in case of fire. But wasn't it too early to worry? After all, it could rain from almost no cloud at all, she had learned from Oregon's playful way with sunshine and flowers. She, for one, was simply going to enjoy the beauty the month had brought. Never had she seen more splendor than the rhododendrons in the hills that hugged the valley.

Almost vain in their glory, the 15-foot-tall shrubs virtually leaned down from the higher elevations, bending with the gentle winds to form floral arches above the roads. Chris Beth filled her galvanized washtubs with armloads of branches that passersby found it necessary to hack off in order to see through the maze of flowers. And still the rhododendrons bloomed on.

But for now the exotic beauty of the settlement had a strong magnetic field. Always spring had restored fidelity to old dreams for her. And this year was especially so. As May's near-summer breezes lifted hay-smells from the tall grass and mingled them with honeysuckle, she felt a sense of wanting to charge ahead. Part of her longed to linger in the dreamlike setting, drinking in its loveliness, listening distantly to the soft-vowel quality of the speech that flowered around her, the potpourri from birds, bees, and neighbors. The other part knew that there must be some sacrifice. Drowsily, this Saturday morning in May, she found herself musing that maybe all progress was bittersweet. One had to let go of one set of values to achieve another.

So it was almost with reluctance that she looked forward to tomorrow's trip. She and Joe would be leaving at four *in the morning* for Willow Grove. What would the church be like, especially its people? And how did they expect her to act? Here there was no reason for concern. Valley folks just accepted and loved "Brother Joseph" and his teacher-wife exactly as they were. Would it be the same in Willow Grove?

Chris Beth stopped folding diapers for little Mart and sat down to think. Already she had prepared enough clothes for the baby to last him a week instead of an extended day. And, even if he ran out of something, Vangie had more than enough. "I guess that's just the way we mothers are, Lord," she murmured.

Mothers! Even yet it was hard to realize the wonder of it all. When, in her infrequent letters, Mama spoke of the "hardship and deprivation you foolish girls have chosen," Chris Beth could only feel a certain pity for her. "Chosen" was hardly the right word. And as for hardships—well, how like her mother to lose herself in some minor detail and miss the miracle.

In the kitchen the clock struck 11. Goodness! She had a way to go...irons to heat to press a dress for tomorrow...Joe's suit to check for buttons...and the singing kettle reminded her that she had better make starch for his Sunday shirt. Better get the coffee going, too. It was almost time for the noon meal.

The big stove gobbled up the firewood she offered, and Chris Beth wiped her brow with the back of her hand. The others were right. It *was* unseasonably hot. It would be nice to let the fire die down, but there was bathwater to heat.

Chris Beth set the coffee to perking and sliced yesterday's leftover ham a little thinner than usual. It was the last in the pork barrel and there was little left of it except the bone for boiling with beans. Of course, meat was no real problem. The speckled trout in Graveyard Creek were one source, and all the neighbors were talking of the salmon run up the river. She remembered with appreciation the smoky succulence of the rick, red-fleshed fish after it had been cured in the underground pits. And, of course, wild game abounded.

But these days a shortage of *anything* bothered Chris Beth more than she admitted to Joe. He had so enjoyed last night's buttermilk pie, and it *had* been especially translucent in appearance and refreshing to the tongue, she thought with pride. Although there was a nice wedge left for today, she decided her husband would enjoy it better if she made no mention that the filling had taken the sugar bin down dangerously low.

It was a blessing that there was no shortage of meal or flour because of the mill. The meal took care of her husband's yen for cornbread. The flour took care of his breakfast sourdough biscuits and the other baking—and, she realized, some other needs as well! For when she started to make starch, there was no more than a scant spoonful remaining in the sack. Well, she would improvise, the way she had seen Mrs. Malone do. Quickly she made a flour paste by adding the boiling water, remembering with a laugh O'Higgin's complaint about his wife's "starchin' me drawers in flour paste, she does, to keep me upright!"

The sound of men's voices reminded Chris Beth that Joe and Wilson had finished the morning's work. But Joe's words caught her off guard. "Enough for two hungry men, Honey?" he called through the window. "We need to get right back to work—"

Whatever else Joe may have said fell on closed ears. Wilson could hardly be called "company," but even family members had a right to be served a proper meal.

Quickly Chris Beth checked the ham. Not enough for two

hungry men. She would have to cut closer to the bone. In her rush not to be detected, she clumsily sliced into the forefinger of her left hand and saw a little spurt of blood run onto her chopping board. Biting her lip to keep from crying out, she sucked at the bleeding finger as she sliced and buttered the salt-rising bread.

"Plenty!" Chris Beth called out cheerfully (mentally adding, "of fried potatoes and buttered carrots, that is!"). Then, making sure the men were not watching as they washed up outside the door, she quickly divided the buttermilk pie in half.

After Joe and Wilson had returned to the mill and she had put little Mart down for a nap, Chris Beth returned to the tasks of preparing for tomorrow's trip to Willow Grove. But she found that her hands were fumbling and her mind was confused. At such times, she knew, it was time to take time out, rest, and pray.

Seated in the quaint old rocker that Joe's mother used to rock him in, Chris Beth raised the window and listened to the laughing of the waterfall. But today it failed to calm her. It seemed to be saying, "Stay...Stay...Stay."

Chris Beth felt tears dangerously close. She closed her eyes. "I don't know how to pray about this, Lord. I just don't know. I want the people to like Joe tomorrow, but if they do, it might mean we'd have to go—" She burst into tears then. "And I want to stay!"

There was still a lot left to be done. She should be working. But instead she sat reviewing her struggles in the settlement, in trying to make a new life for herself and for the others she loved so much. It had been so hard. So *very* hard.

"But it's all worth it—more than worth it," she mused aloud. "Joe. Little Mart. Warm friendships for myself and Vangie. And love. Most of all, *love!* Without all this I might never have rediscovered God—"

Fear clutched her heart at the thought of what the settlement meant to her. Then more tears rolled off her cheeks, and with them a little moan.

"It's me again, Lord, with another problem—the biggest one yet. Please, *please*, don't let it all be taken away now!"

15

Willow Grove

Chris Beth had been too preoccupied with her own thoughts to wonder how a team of horses could possibly find a narrow road in the predawn darkness. As she sat close to Joe, thankful for the warmth of the worn lap robe he had thoughtfully tucked around her feet and legs, she asked, "Can they see?"

"A little, but they go more by instinct."

"I could use a little of that myself."

"Scared?" Joe's voice was quiet but concerned.

"Maybe. I've never ridden at night without lights—"

"It will be light soon or I'd have hung the lanterns in front. We're heading east, by the way, in the general direction of Portland. You'll see some new country."

Were there animals there?

Well, yes. Lots of deer and elk—even geese, ducks, quail, Chinese pheasants...grouse...and did she know what Hungarian partridges were?

She did not. But she was more interested in the possibility of wolves, bears, and cougars.

Could be, Joe admitted. But, he insisted, "Could be doesn't mean *are.*"

True, but the feel of a cold steel object lying between the two of them told Chris Beth that the possibility was very real. Why else would Joe have brought the shotgun? She wished for Esau, but Joe was right, of course, in saying it would be too long a day for the dog. He'd have to sit in the buggy so long while they were in the church. She fell into an uneasy silence.

"Doze if you can," he advised, pulling her head gently

onto his shoulder. And maybe she would have—she was so weary from the days of preparation—but just as she was on the edge of slumber, the tinkle of a bell—and then dozens, or was it hundreds—broke the eerie silence.

"Joe," she whispered, "sheep?"

Joe stopped the buggy with a jolt. "Sit right where you are."

Without answering her question, Joe jumped out and disappeared into the predawn darkness. She was alone, alone, *alone*.

What could be going on? Why had he left her here when he knew she was afraid? When she whispered Joe's name there was no answer. Maybe Wilson was right in saying she was no match for this country. Maybe she *was* the fragile "Southern belle" he had gently poked fun at when she first came. She stiffened at the thought. That was a long time ago, and just because she longed for the security of the cabin right now didn't mean she couldn't cope! She would show him and Joe—as she had shown Mama—she would show them over and over—

But the sudden rattle of brush near her side of the buggy dissolved her resolution. "Joe!" she cried out before she could stop herself.

"Right here," Joe said softly, and Chris Beth could hear him picking his way through the darkness. Then, to her immense relief, his familiar form loomed through the darkness, which seemed to thicken every second. At least they were together, no matter what the danger.

Joe climbed in beside her. "There's a little pullout just a way ahead. We'll have to hurry. Road's not wide enough for them to get past." Even his whisper seemed to echo in the stillness.

"Them?" The word sounded hollow in her ears.

"Freight wagons—Mariettas, most likely, the kind drawn by six spans of horses. It's the bell teams you're hearing, our signal to make way."

Fear clutched her heart as the team responded to Joe's "Giddyup!" and moved forward—in the direction of the approaching wagons! If only Joe would break the silence—touch her, even—but he was silent.

Clang! *Clang!* The bells were louder, as were the hoarse voices that sang lustily. Chris Beth scarcely breathed. Then the unmistakable smell of horseflesh and something she could only imagine as carnage told her that the men were within a stone's throw. And then she was overcome with a wave of nausea. The smell, *the awful smell!*

"What—?" But before she could finish her whispered question, Joe's hand closed over her mouth.

And then she realized that the revelers were right along-side the buggy. For one horrible moment, the wagons slowed as if to stop. Then, at the crack of a whip, they picked up speed once they were past the curve of the turn-out in the road.

When Joe did not speak, Chris Beth ventured shakily, "Th-the smell?"

Her question seemed anticlimactic, but it was the best she could come up with. Her adrenalin slowed. But she felt totally exhausted.

"Pelts," Joe answered matter-of-factly. It was a relief to hear him speak in a normal voice. "Usually the wagons return to Redding empty after the haul."

"Of what?"

"Supplies. Immigrants. All bound for Portland. Sometimes it's gold. But the skins are about as valuable as gold itself. You'll get used to all this."

She doubted it! "Are they always so noisy and—and frightening?"

Joe reached to pat her hand. She wished he would take her in his arms, but the stop had slowed their timing, she supposed. He took the reins in both hands and then answered, "They're a pretty rough-and-ready bunch—mostly boozed up on the return trip. Most act civilized if there are womenfolk along."

Chris Beth shuddered at the thought of travel-weary im-migrant women making the long journey westward under such conditions. And she had thought a stagecoach primi-tive! Even this morning's encounter shook her new-found confidence, and she wished again for the security of the cabin. Ordinarily they would be getting up about this time. Joe would have a warm fire going, and together they would watch little Mart, all rosy with sleep, yawn his infant "Good morning!" She was homesick. That's what she was. Just a few miles away from the settlement, and already homesick!

"Giddyup!" Joe clucked his tongue again, then said to Chris Beth, "We'll have to clip along to make up for lost time. The trail's going to be rough from here on, too."

"That's all right," she said stoutly—a comment she was to regret as the trail grew more narrow and dusty. It was a relief to see a few windows light up here and there, but cabins were far apart and often far from the rutted road. Finally they seemed to recede into the shadows of mountains which even the promise of sunrise did not seem to light up.

The coffee would be bubbling away happily now and the sourdough biscuits ready to pop into the oven. *Stop it*, she said fiercely to herself.

"Tell me about Willow Grove," she encouraged Joe, more to get her mind off home than because of interest in their destination. But as he talked, Chris Beth found herself keenly interested.

"First of all, we need to get to know these people and their ways. Little Mart's parents were among their followers." She nodded, remembering only that the young Mrs. Martin was reserved, said to be well-educated, and wore black dresses that were collared and cuffed in white. She touched her own dove-gray cotton with its little nosegays of pink roses and wondered if her apparel would be out of place. Joe had said, "Something cool for this unusual May weather—and your umbrella." She hoped Joe had picked up her pink umbrella by the door—not that she could do much about either matter now. She would rather hear more about Willow Grove anyway.

"Do they worship like we do in the settlement?"

"Services vary, depending on lots of things." Chris Beth had a feeling he was hedging and was reasonably sure of it when he added, "At least they have a building." A real church! That would be nice. If *that* were the only difference—

"I know, too, that they didn't take to the circuit riders.

Too emotional, they said, and," he chuckled, "violent."

"Violent? *Jonas?*" She asked of the preacher who had married them.

"No, Noah Somebody—I guess he was quite a character. The congregation, 13 of them, I hear, called themselves 'disciples' and said they only needed a quiet leader who knew how to break bread but not their silence." Joe chuckled as if remembering something funny—or to divert her. But she was not to be diverted.

"You mean he wasn't supposed to *preach?*"

"Something like that, but that was a long time ago. They've probably changed the requirements. D-don't worry about it, Chrissy."

Her husband's stammering told her that he was worrying enough for both of them. She shifted the subject.

"You were laughing at something."

Joe threw his head back and laughed heartily before sharing the anecdote that had made its way from community to community in the new land. "The story goes that Noah was dubbed a 'sundowner' by just about every group he visited. He seemed to reach one of the worshiper's houses right at sundown, then pointed out that it would be cruel for them to refuse him bed and board for the night what with the wolf at the door, so to speak."

It was good to see that Joe had relaxed. As he went on to describe the this Noah fellow, Chris Beth wondered if there wasn't a bit of the man's personality deep inside Joe himself. It wasn't a new thought, really. Gentle though he was, there was a strength to Joe that seemed to need testing and tempering. She hoped he would continue so she could gain more insight. And he did.

"He made quite a name for himself—said to have baptized more than 3000 converts, some kind of record among the circuit riders."

"Well-educated?"

Joe shook his head. "But bright! Knew the entire Bible by heart and quoted it by memory. Miss Mollie heard him preach once and said he couldn't have read the Bible he owned anyway, as he 'beat it to pieces tryin' to pound the Word in!' "

"Sounds like Mrs. Malone," Chris Beth laughed. "Did she say what this man looked like, this supposedly violent preacher?"

"Big and strong, and took no foolishness. Some roughneck came to the meetinghouse one night and started making trouble. Noah supposedly left the pulpit and threw him out bodily. But what I was laughing about was his contribution to politics—" Joe paused to look her direction, "Am I boring you?"

"Oh no! I'm enjoying every minute." (*And I wonder if you know how much*, she thought, for she was seeing not a new man but one who fleshed out more and more each day.)

"Well, if you're sure—just one story more and then we'll take a break." Goodness knows she needed that, but she needed to hear Joe's story even more.

"One of the legislators decided that once Oregon was a state and no longer a territory, there ought to be a chaplain. The only preacher around was old Noah, and they all dreaded him. He was noted for his long-winded sermons. But he surprised them! The men prepared themselves for a long, loud prayer. What they got was one of his favorite passages: 'Father, forgive them for they know not what they do!' "

Even as the two of them laughed together, Chris Beth knew that Joe was sharing with her a need, possibly unrecognized by himself, to make use of his inner self—to minister to people the way he felt the Lord intended. Maybe Willow Grove would be right, but what he had told her made her wonder. And they *did* have to be practical, too. Even ministers had to support their families.

"Joe," she hesitated, then—encouraged by his listening nod—continued: "Joe, can these people at Willow Grove afford a resident minister? They must have paid Noah as well as fed him."

"Well, yes and no—about paying Noah, that is. He took in a lot of money from some of the churches." Joe laughed again. "He made friends with the owner of a saloon-keeper up north—even baptized him, and then encouraged the man to bring his 'talent' with him!"

Talent? Yes, Joe explained, that of raking in cash. "He

would just lock the doors and refuse 'leavin' rights' until Noah's big black hat was full." *How awful!* Yes, Joe admitted, but the notorious circuit rider built a lot of churches that way. Some even thought that, secretly, some of the funds for the Willow Grove Church may have come from Noah's coffer. Well, today should be very interesting. But her question about a resident minister remained.

Joe reined in at the next turnout. The shade of the fir trees looked inviting, for the sun had grown hot already. "Salmonberries are ripe!" Joe, pointing excitedly to the giant red-orange berries, failed to see how stiff and lame Chris Beth was from the long ride as he helped her down and offered her a juicy berry.

She scarcely tasted it. She was too buried in putting together a picture of Willow Creek. Already an alien world had opened along the way. But in a sense she dreaded the uncertainty ahead even more. What would the church be like? And what would it do to their lives?

16

Upon This Rock

Chris Beth wondered if she had a muscle anywhere in her that didn't ache from fatigue as she tried to align herself in order to enter the church with a measure of dignity. Joe made no complaint, but he looked tired. He took her arm wordlessly as they neared the door, and wordlessly she smiled in appreciation. Then she inhaled deeply, hoping to ease the tremor inside her being.

At least it was good to see a church building again, one with a spire! It wasn't so tall, but it reached toward the heavens all the same. And it was good to see real panes of glass in the windows. But there ought to be some sign of welcome, some little show of warmth, someone there to greet them. An open door, or even the sound of music or song from inside.

Joe's large hand fumbled with the latch. Chris Beth disengaged her hand from his elbow, and then she saw that he was hesitating.

"Are you ready, Chr-Chrissy?" he asked in a low, uncertain voice.

After the long ride, the gray dress probably looked like it hung from a peg. She tried to smooth the soft folds. As for her hair, earlier she had drawn it smoothly from her forehead, but by now—

"Do I look a fright?" she asked anxiously.

"You look fine," Joe said without looking. "I meant, are you r-ready for this—if—?"

Joe didn't finish. There was no need. She knew the question—the same one that lay in her own heart. *Ready for this? Oh, Joe, I don't know if I'm ready for this church or any other outside the security of the settlement. Don't you know that?*

"But you're only here to see, aren't you? Then decide?"

"That's part of it. But these people decide, too. And you!" He turned to face her. "You do—do understand, Chrissy, that I *have* to preach? That there's no decision about that?"

And the place doesn't matter. But she forced a tight smile. "Like Noah?"

Joe studied her face, then smiled in gentle conspiracy. "Like Noah," he whispered. "Only my way."

Then she must try to understand.

There was no time to think further. Joe opened the door cautiously. It was dark inside the church in spite of the windows. For a moment she wondered foolishly if there were a congregation. And it was so quiet that she and Joe might well have been alone. When her eyes adjusted to the shadowy darkness, Chris Beth saw that all heads were covered with black, giving a strange feeling of mourning. None of the worshipers lifted bowed heads as she and Joe entered. Could they all have gone to sleep waiting for them to arrive?

What do we do? Her eyes asked Joe. His slight palms-up gesture signaled back, *I don't know.*

When, in due time, one of the men stood, and—with eyes closed—began to speak softly, Joe motioned her to be seated in one of the straight-backed, homemade pews. The speaker's voice was so muted that it was hard to hear his words. And when he sat down, another man stood, and then another. *They must be giving testimonials,* she thought.

Maybe her own head should be bowed, but Chris Beth was unable to resist looking at her strange surroundings and the equally strange people in it. The women all looked alike, at least to an outsider, she thought. The similarity went beyond the dark clothing. It was in their faces, so unreadable and expressionless. It was hard to tell whether the immobility of the women's features spelled quiet desperation or serenity.

And the men! Why, they looked like rows and rows of prophets, lined up the way they were, eyes either cast downward or staring upward with a glazed expression. In their unbelievably long beards, they reminded Chris Beth of the mossy oak trees in her southern home.

Chris Beth was suddenly aware of a prolonged silence. She glanced at Joe questioningly. He smiled in response. Then, as if seeking support, he squeezed her hand before he rose and, to her surprise, made his way down the dim aisle to stand before the group.

Seeming to take a cue from the others, Joe spoke softly. "Upon this rock I—I build my church—" he began.

She had heard him use the text before. Even under normal circumstances, it was not one of his better sermons. Today it seemed to convey no message at all. The words sounded empty. And Joe was stuttering badly.

"Th-the church s-spoken of here is—is the human h-heart. And it—it m-must be centered upon Jesus Ch-Christ—"

Oh, Joe, my darling, her heart cried out, *it's not an inspired sermon. They aren't even listening! You can never be a Noah here—*

She squeezed her eyes shut and, without warning, the curtain in her mind parted. The scene around her dissolved. Joe's voice floated away. And she was transported to some future state. Hammers pounded. Saws whined. And, above it all, there was the sound of singing. And then a voice *(O'Higgin's?)* saying, "We'll observe the Lord's Supper by candlelight. Here! *Upon this rock!* Until the buildin' be finished!"

17

Pancakes at Midnight

The trip home was long and hard. There were times when Chris Beth longed to cry out, "I can't go any further!" Once, long ago, somebody had told her that she couldn't be hungry and scared at the same time, but that wasn't true! She was starving and she was scared out of her wits.

Surely the fir trees hadn't been this dense just this morning. It had been dark then, too, but in her mind there was a difference between morning-dark and night-dark. This was so *total!* This morning the predators of the night had been finishing their shift. Now they were just beginning. Coyotes were calling hungrily from all directions, their wails of despair sending a chill down her spine. Once she had been sure that the deeper, more throaty howl was that of a wolf. She regretted having asked Joe. Uncertainty would have been better than knowing.

"That was a mating call—nothing to fear," Joe had tried to reassure her. "It's only the *packs* that sometimes are a threat to man." Well, cougars weren't like that. One was all it took. She squeezed her hands tightly in her lap and tried to think of something else.

But the "Whoo—owwwww! Who, who, who, whooo-oow!" hoots of the watching owls would allow her no peace. When she felt one of the night creatures glide effortlessly by—and seem to hover on silent wings right over their heads—she let out a little cry in spite of herself.

"It's only an owl," Joe soothed, pulling her closer to his side.

" 'An abomination among fowl,' some say. Who ever called them wise?"

"I, for one! Just look what the fellow did for me—brought you snuggling up close."

"I'd have snuggled anyway. I'm cold."

"Shucks! And here I thought it was my fatal charm."

"That too," she giggled, moving a little closer still.

"I guess the owls are hungry like two others I know of, hmmm?"

Chris Beth laughed. "I wasn't going to complain, but I'm caved in completely. Of course, it's been—what, 18 hours between meals?"

Joe inhaled deeply. "You don't need to tell me that my sermon, if you could call it that, wasn't what the Willow Grove people hoped for." When she made no answser, he continued, "But it ought to please 'em that we're fasting right along with their tradition!"

Well, they might as well treat the matter lightly. It wasn't going to do them in to go without food this long. It was more that it was so unexpected to find the worshipers spending the Lord's Day fasting and meditating instead of singing praise and celebrating at the Lord's Table, either in communion or at an after-church picnic.

"I should have eaten my oatmeal this morning."

Joe leaned to kiss her forehead. "I promise you a real breakfast when we get home."

"At midnight?"

"Does it matter?"

"No." Nothing mattered right now—not even the disappointments of the day—except that they were together and that Joe wasn't as discouraged as she thought he might be. Actually, she decided, he seemed relieved, almost jubilant.

Since that was his mood, there was no reason why they could not discuss the day openly. She was glad about that.

"Did the men say anything after the meeting?"

"Very little. Mostly they talked about fear that there will be poor crops if the drought continues. They use grain as their medium more than money, I think. Sort of a common storehouse arrangement."

She understood that but wondered what they did for cash. Turned grain in (sort of like the miners did gold), Joe supposed. But for paying a preacher? Joe said he suspected that they took care of their leader with food.

"Did any of the women talk with you?" Joe asked.

"Just nodded. I gather they say nothing in church?"

"Apparently. I don't think they intended to be unkind."

Chris Beth hadn't gathered that either. Just shy, and in keeping with what they thought a woman's place ought to be. She had noticed, however, their unusual pattern of speech when they spoke to the children: "Get thee into the wagon...has thou forgotten thy manners?"

"And the men *did* look a little like rows and rows of prophets marching down the aisles, didn't they?" Chris Beth asked, remembering the unbelievably long beards that they all wore.

"Tradition seems important. Different from my own practices. But they are sincere people. I could feel that."

Chris Beth had felt that, too, and found herself thinking that she was sure they would come through in time of crisis.

"Tell you what," Joe said as he helped her from the buggy. "You run in and get into something snuggly and warm. Brush your hair and—would you mind letting it hang loose?"

"Why, Joe—Brother Joseph!"

"Well, it occurs to me that the bride and groom have never had a night alone since that little stint right after the vows."

"But what about that breakfast?" she teased.

"This one's on me! First a fire. Then I feed the horses and my wife."

Strange that all the fears of the day seemed silly now. Outside, darkness cloaked the cabin. But there were no pockets in the night from which highwaymen and wild animals could emerge and then pounce! It was a kind of starstruck darkness that spoke of warmth and peace of mind.

Languidly—and for some reason, happily—Chris Beth unwound her dark braids and brushed her hair until the red glints came back. As she was about to follow the unmistakable aroma of coffee and buttermilk pancakes, she turned and smiled into the darkness.

18

Bearing of Gifts—And Burdens

Two weeks after the trip to Willow Grove, two of the "disciples" paid the Craigs an unexpected visit. Chris Beth was pitting cherries for a cobbler when an unfamiliar voice called from the front gate, "Hello, hello! May we enter in?"

Joe, Wilson, and young Wil were setting out tomato plants on the little section of land they called the "island" down by the creek.

"Soil's sandier there and retains the water. Maybe the plants will grow in spite of the heat," Joe had said. She hoped so, for they were going to need all the garden produce possible to tide them over until one or more of the two family members could be back on some kind of payroll. The babies were growing like weeds and seemed to thrive under any conditions (unlike the domestic plants). And young Wil was in need of shoes and a few school supplies come fall. The rest of them could manage, barring some emergency. Of course, emergencies *did* arise when least expected.

Hurriedly Chris Beth looked out the cabin window and, recognizing the men by their dark clothing, opened the door. "Do come in!" she invited, unlatching the door. Then, remembering that she wore a long apron over her floor-length skirt, Chris Beth pulled it over her head, dried her wet hands on it, and dropped it into Joe's easy chair in the corner he reserved for a study.

Silently the two men came up the petunia-bordered walk side by side. She wondered foolishly if they would try to enter the doorway in the same fashion. She doubted if it would accommodate both men, even though they were sparse of frame. But at the door the gentleman on the right stepped formally behind his companion and bowed with the words "Brother Amos." Brother Amos stepped ahead at the signal, then lifted his hat to his hostess and said politely, "Mrs. Craig, this is my Christian brother, Brother Benjamin."

Chris Beth nodded to the two men, bade them sit down, and offered coffee. Brother Amos and Brother Benjamin looked surprised. "No, thank you. We do not partake," they said in unison.

Oh, dear, she thought, *I've done something wrong!* What could she offer? Maybe some cold cider? But before there was an opportunity to phrase the offer, Brother Amos said, "Water will be sufficient."

In the kitchen Chris Beth set out glasses and then "yoo-hooed" to Joe. At her call Joe came running. Shaking her head to indicate there was no problem, she put a warning finger to her lips and whispered, "The 'disciples'! Fetch cold water from the spring."

When she reentered the front room, both men stood. "We bear gifts," said Brother Amos. "Wouldst thou receive them?"

"I would be honored," she said, wondering if that was the right response.

By the time Joe had come in and shaken hands with the two men, Chris Beth had poured them tall glasses of fresh, cold water. She excused herself and, while Brother Amos spoke in low tones with Joe, Brother Benjamin made the first of several trips to the two pack mules they obviously had ridden the long distance. It was terribly hot. They must be exhausted, Chris Beth thought.

Admittedly they were strange, but something about them touched her deeply. And it warmed her heart to see that her husband was talking openly with Brother Amos.

"Lord," she whispered, "I find something more to love in this wonderful man every day!" Unconsciously she hummed as she popped the cobbler into the oven. She had little more than tidied up the kitchen when Joe told her from the door that their guests had refused his invitation to supper.

"I'm sorry," she said truthfully as she went in to say good-bye. Then, before she could stop herself, she gasped, "What on earth—?"

For there, in the middle of the room, stood sacks of all the whole-grain breads, cookies, and cakes that she could name—and then some. How could they have known that her sugar bin was all but empty? To hide her tears of gratitude, Chris Beth hurried out into the pantry to bring them honey and jars of her favorite wild plum jelly.

"I just wish there were more I could do," she said.

"There is," said Brother Amos. "Thou canst pray for rain. My brother and I have had a vision. The drought is the first of our several plagues. Wouldst thou and thy house help bear our burdens?"

"Indeed, we will!" Joe assured Brother Amos. The two "disciples" raised their hands as if in benediction, having brought all they had to offer.

19

The Second Plague

Joe showed no disappointment at there being no monetary offer for him at Willow Grove. Instead, he seemed almost relieved. However, the two of them agreed that the encounter had been a blessing. "And we're to meet again, you know."

"Really? When?" Chris Beth was very surprised.

"Brother Amos said some of the members will be with us Sunday at the brush arbor—praying for rain, you know."

"Joe," she said slowly, "is it really that serious?"

"It will be unless there is rain soon. Everything depends on rain in the Oregon Country. Crops. The mill. Possibility of more waterways opening for shipping..." Joe paused as if wanting to say more, then almost to himself he added, "...timber."

She had taken this too casually. Here she was worried about summer gardens and little Mart's prickly heat when their entire way of life was at stake. It simply had not occurred to Chris Beth that the beautiful timber needed water. Yes, they must pray. And she must keep Joe's spirits up.

So there was an air of festivity on Sunday when the Craigs and the Norths boarded the buggy. If Dobbin and Battle felt that four adults, two babies, one growing boy, and the basket of honey and breads was an overload for two horses, they took it in stride. Seeming to sense the attempted lightheartedness of their family, the team clopped along at a pace that belied their years.

"*Oh*, but it's good to be home!" Chris Beth said happily.

The others laughed. "Makes one appreciate home to be gone so long," Wilson teased. "Like one day!"

87

"It was a *long* day," she defended.

The men began talking in low tones then, and Chris Beth was able to catch little of the conversation. She thought Wilson said something about going to Portland to see a publisher. Maybe that meant he had completed his book... but wasn't he saying something about setting up an office? Did that mean so far away, and did Vangie know? Either way, her sister apparently had heard none of the talk this Sunday morning. For, taking advantage of the men's talking, she had whispered, "How do I look? Any different?"

Chris Beth surveyed her with admiration. Vangie always looked beautiful. Her delicate features, almost marblelike in their smoothness, and her silver-blonde hair, which always looked as if each strand were backlighted by sunlight, gave her the look of a visiting angel. But, as usual, she felt a nagging concern for the younger girl. It seemed to Chris Beth that Vangie looked more delicate with each passing day.

"You're lovely. You have a way of making anything you wear look new!" she answered Vangie's question.

Vangie was delighted. "You *did* notice! The reason the dress looks new is," she paused to lower her voice modestly, "I was able to get into my corset today!"

She was unaware that the horses had slowed down for the bend of the road leading to the arbor and that the men had paused in their conversation. "You and who else?" Wilson called over his shoulder. "I see, Joe, why they chose to ride back there!"

"Wilson!" Vangie's cheeks were pink. "Don't you dare—"

Wilson was enjoying himself. And suddenly so was Chris Beth. It was like old times—no matter what lay ahead.

"Found my bride strapped to the bed post, I vow to you, trying to take her own life by strangulation—around the waist!"

"*Wilson!*" Vangie wailed. "This seating promised privacy."

Young Wil was enjoying himself immensely. Then, to Chris Beth's surprise, Joe chimed in, "Isn't there a better way of having our ladies look wasp-waisted? I've meant to ask Chrissy."

Chris Beth put a warning finger to her lips. After all, they were nearing the church. Brother Joseph, his teacher-wife, Doctor Wil, and his wife (wasn't she a nurse?) were expected to maintain a certain air of dignity. But she did whisper, "You find a way, Brother Joseph, and we'll all be rich!"

Usually Chris Beth would have been viewing the scenery. She just never seemed to tire of Oregon's panorama of beauty, no matter what the season. Today there had been so much banter that she had failed to notice that some of the sheen had gone from the leaves of the laurel and manzanita bushes and that the needles of her beloved fir trees looked dusty and tired.

She did notice, though, that the brush on the arbor had curled and twisted in the hot sun. So many of the leaves and needles had dropped from the boughs that the sun had found its way to the dirt floors. Not that the condition of the temporary roof made any difference in attendance. Indeed, it had doubled or more just since Sunday before last.

Neighbors swarmed to meet the buggy, and Chris Beth saw from the corner of her eye that the Muslin City people had gathered beneath the arbor. The Chu family stood just outside as if awaiting an invitation. She must get to them quickly, although she doubted if there would be seating space. And then she saw Mrs. Malone—leave it to her to find a solution—engineering the spreading of quilts and blankets, taken from wagonbeds, for the late-arriving guests. And still they came!

Chris Beth turned to Joe to flash a message of appreciation, but Brother Amos (and what appeared to be a dozen others in the same somber black-and-white attire) had approached. Joe, bless him, was shaking hands and introducing the men to Nate Goldsmith, who took over with a flourish as Joe made his way to the pulpit.

Joe prayed for the presence of the Lord. And surely the Lord answered his prayer. It was evidenced in the singing (the "disciples" took no part, but they gave no indication of offense). It was further evidenced in Joe's inspired sermon (so different, Chris Beth thought, from last Sunday's!). But, most of all, it was evidenced in the general feeling of fellowship. Despite differences of race, creed, color, and forms of worship, there was a common bond of love.

"Am I right, Lord, in thinking Joe is helping You create this bond?" And, deep in her heart, it was as if the Lord said, "Yes."

Chris Beth felt the presence of the Lord in their midst even more when Joe invited all to join in a prayer for rain. Many of the men rose at the invitation and walked up to kneel at the altar. Some of those remaining behind, having given their seats to women and children, knelt just outside the brush arbor. Most of the women remained where they were and, with heads bowed, offered silent prayers. Only the Willow Grove guests rose, raised both hands imploringly, and fixed their gaze upon something seemingly invisible to the eyes of those around them.

The farmers prayed one by one, then waited for Joe to offer the benediction. Chris Beth always loved this part. Joe's words were invariably the same: "The Lord bless you and keep you. The Lord make His face to shine upon you—"

But today he seemed to hesitate, as if waiting for something. And it came. Brother Amos, still standing, began in a soft monotone which at first Chris Beth was unable to hear. Straining to catch the words, she unconsciously opened her eyes and looked into the face of the visiting "disciple." What she saw made it impossible to close her lids again.

The speaker, whose near-transparent skin was etched with soft creases—not the deep ones she would expect from a man who had endured so much sun—wore the look of an ethereal being. His wide-open eyes, a deep blue that only very old people or babies seemed to have, were fixed in a trancelike stare. The lips kept moving...moving... until finally words were distinguishable.

"...And where there is one, there will be more, and more, then hordes. Ah, yes, my brothers, we saw it happen in Utah. And we shall see it again. We have brought you the signs."

All heads lifted then as Brother Amos held out his handful of grasshoppers. "The second of the plagues..." his voice trailed away.

● ● ●

"Strange they didn't stay for dinner, what with that long ride back to Willow Grove," Mrs. Malone said after the "disciples" had made a hasty departure.

"They fast on Sunday," Chris Beth explained as she helped the other women weight the tablecloths down against a possible wind.

"*Ach!* Tell that to mine *bon* ol' man!" Olga Goldsmith said tartly.

Rachel Beltran moved closer to Chris Beth. "Been thinkin' 'bout them grasshoppers. Know 'bout that, too?"

"No," Chris Beth admitted slowly, aware that the eyes of all the other women were focused on her. "It was news to me too, and I don't know what to make of it. I do know that these are devout men. And somehow I don't take this lightly."

"They don't know any more'n we do!" Bertie Solomon declared, picking up a covered bowl and tugging at the lid.

"Now, now, Bertie, they jest might," Mrs. Malone said. "They jest might."

The bowl slipped from Mrs. Solomon's hand and bounced onto the white cloth below, spilling the shredded cabbage. She stooped to scrape up the contents. "I refuse t' believe it and that's that."

The men came then, and they too were talking about the possibility that there might be "a mite of truth" to what "them peculiar men" said.

"Me, I ain't losin' sleep over it," Nate said in a tone that boasted courage. "Still 'n all, I wonder jest how we'd recognize a real, honest-to-goodness prophet. Any ideas 'fore blessin' this food fer our bodies, Brother Joseph?"

"We'll know it was a real prophecy if it comes to pass, won't we?" Joe asked quietly.

A strange silence fell over the group.

20

Fulfillment of the Prophecy

Both Chris Beth and Vangie cried when Joe and Wilson left for Portland. "You'll be all right, Darling," Joe hugged Chris Beth. "I wouldn't leave you except that—well, you know why."

Yes, she knew. How well she knew! It was mid-June and the heat hung like a thing alive over the settlement. The gardens had failed miserably. The only hope of canning lay with the peach, pear, and apple orchards. The wheat looked promising because it could survive with less water, but the corn hadn't made it.

What it all amounted to was that Joe must be on the look-out for a church, even if it meant moving far away from the people she loved—far away from the very spot where Joe felt called to do the Lord's work, and far away from the dreams they had promised themselves, each other, and the Lord.

But knowing did not stem the tide of tears. "It's just—just that we—we've never been apart. And the two months seem so short—"

"A lifetime seems too short together," Joe whispered understandingly. "That's why there is eternity."

"But first there's life here!" Chris Beth objected.

When Joe turned to face her, love lighted his eyes so that the gold flecks showed through. But his voice chided gently. "Yes, there's life here. And I never underestimate its value, Darling. Quite the contrary! It's because of the brevity of our little mortal span that we have to work hard at following the will of the Lord."

"You mean the ministry, don't you?"

"In my case, yes. In yours—oh, Chrissy, don't you know how important it is that I have you with me all the way—*here* and *there?* Don't you know how much I love you and need your help to do what I must?"

Chris Beth bit her lip to hold back the tears. Yes, she knew. And she wasn't going to cry. Was she? *Yes, she was!*

How on earth, she wondered, *do women without wonderful Christian husbands survive? Who reassures them? Makes them know that everything here and hereafter will be all right?*

"Young Wil will be with you. He's becoming quite a man, you know."

She nodded through her tears. It wasn't as if she would be alone. There were little Mart...Vangie...True...and Esau. Not alone—no—but *lonely.* Why, she wouldn't even be a whole person without Joe.

Joe touched the back of her neck where the dark tendrils curled with perspiration. "Wilson's waiting," he reminded her gently.

She walked with him to where Wilson stood beside the two saddled horses. Vangie, she knew from experience, would be sobbing her heart out, her face buried in the biggest feather pillow she could find. But Chris Beth felt an urgent need to gain control of herself, to show Joe she *was* developing into the kind of pioneer woman he needed to fulfill his ministry, and to wave until he was out of sight. She squared her shoulders bravely and hoped her voice was steady. "Good luck on the book, Wilson. I'll look after Vangie. And the Lord bless both of you!"

Turning, she was about to run into the house and let go of a few more tears when she caught sight of young Wil leaning against one of the twin fir trees just outside the slat fence around the cabin. His shoulders were convulsing with sobs.

Ashamed of her thoughtlessness, Chris Beth ran to the boy. Of course he had wanted to go with the men! Why, a trip by horseback to Portland would have been a lark. She squatted beside the small figure, wondering what to say. But he spoke first, "I wanna be a man!"

"Well, now, your being the man of the house this week

will prove you're on your way," she said, trying not to sound patronizing.

Young Wil made a helpless gesture. "That's not what I mean."

He had dark eyes, so like Wilson's, but pale hair—like straw. His usually smooth skin was sprinkled with a few blemishes now, bearing out what his behavior told: adolescence. It was a boy pleading for help—sullenly.

Patience. Patience. "Just what *do* you mean?" she asked calmly. When there was no answer, she extended her question. "You mean, I think, that you wish something big would happen. The kind of thing that makes one into an instant hero?"

"Yeah!" young Wil said without thinking. Then, looking sheepish, he added, "Shucks! I didn't mean that—not exactly."

"But *I* have felt that way!"

"You have?" He was all attention.

"Lots of times," she admitted, wishing it were not true.

"Name one," young Wil begged, his liquid eyes no longer sullen.

"Well, now—" She pretended to think, and they both laughed. "Today!" Taking advantage of his change of mood, she hurried on, "Yes, this very day I'd like to be Chicken Little so I could run and tell the news!"

"That the sky's falling?" Young Wil, a child again, giggled.

"The same. And you know what? I've a feeling that before the week's over, you'll get your chance."

The boy studied his bare feet. "You always understand me," he said, "like you were my own—" To Chris Beth's disappointment, he checked the words. "But, Miss Chrissy—"

"Chrissy to you, Wil."

"Chrissy," he said without hesitation, "the sky *wasn't* falling."

"You're right," she said slowly. "Help me remember that, will you?"

• • •

The grasshoppers came the next day. Chris Beth had built

a fire beneath the black, three-legged, iron washpot in the backyard of the Big House early in preparation for boiling the white clothing. Young Wil was bringing rinsewater from the spring. And Vangie was tending the bees when the first of the insects came, as if by chance, on silent wings. The hens stopped dusting themselves beneath the shade of the row of sunflowers in the garden and did away with the invaders in short order.

"Good riddance to them, girls," Chris Beth said to the lady fowl.

Later she wondered why she felt no real foreboding at the appearance of the first of the hoppers. She had been more disturbed than she cared to admit when Brother Amos had presented the grasshoppers in such a dramatic way several weeks before. And, even though some of the other settlers tried to light-touch the prophecy, she sensed that they too were upset by the very suggestion that even a few of the creatures were hereabouts.

Wilson had suggested that Boston Buck and the rest of the Indians would have a field day, since one of their confessed loves was for grasshopper cakes! And Nate Goldsmith had teasingly proclaimed it to be the Year of the Grasshopper.

Fiddle! What did he know? Mrs. Malone had wondered.

Got it from Mr. Chu, O'Higgin had chimed in—something to do with the Chinese New Year or *Poor Richard's Almanac.*

The conversation ended when Miss Mollie gave him a withering look and said, "A week ago it was the Week of the Rabbit because you caught one in the remains of the garden. Then 'twas the Year of the Leprechaun 'cause you couldn't find both your socks. Men!"

But deep down Chris Beth sensed that Brother Amos's warning held some credibility.

It was young Wil who first noticed a faint whir in the morning stillness. "Do you hear it?" the boy asked Chris Beth as he finished hauling the rinsewater.

She listened. Yes, she did. "Help yourself to cornbread sticks. Butter's in the cooler. I'll see if Joe and Wilson left something running in the mill."

Everything seemed in order when Chris Beth entered the cool, damp building, shut up tight the way she would have expected. Any sound coming from the mill would have been drowned out by the noise of the waterfall anyway, she realized once she was inside. But what a relief to be in the building with the machinery not grinding away. So quiet. So restful. And so cool to her warm skin. When her eyes adjusted to the dark, she noticed an empty barrel—just begging, it seemed, to be sat upon! The fire would be blazing. The washwater would be boiling. But young Wil was on hand in case the baby woke up. So, for one luxurious moment, she would rest....

She had slept little last night. The bed was so empty without Joe. She had taken little Mart from the cradle and cuddled him close, but, comforting as the round little body was, she had been afraid to doze for fear she would roll on the baby.

"I'm so tired," she said aloud, "maybe ten minutes worth of rest will do no harm—"

Chris Beth awoke with a start. Tired or not, she had not expected to sleep this morning! She struggled to her feet, and, her eyes still glazed with slumber, hurried toward the door.

There she was startled by a buzz and then a roar that pounded against her eardrums as she pushed at the iron latch. When the heavy door yielded to her weight and the door opened a crack, she was even more startled by the absence of light! How could clouds have come so quickly? Still not thinking clearly, Chris Beth hoped for rain.

But before she was able to scan the sky some objects struck her face with a stinging blow, followed by another and another. And, suddenly to her horror, she was attacked from all directions—by what she was unable to tell. She only knew that her face was stinging and burning...that she was blinded...and then that her entire body was weighted by the driving force. "Oh, no!" she gasped as she stepped outside.

For, although she dared not open her eyes, the awful truth came, and with it revulsion. Fear turned to terror. *Grasshoppers!*

In an effort to breathe, Chris Beth covered her face with the apron she wore, taking a deep breath. Panic was her worst enemy. Stay calm. She strained her numbed senses in an effort to recall how far and in which direction she was from either house. Then she wondered if Vangie had made it back from the beehives. She must check...no, it was best to wait inside the mill until the hordes of insects passed. But before reaching the door, it creaked shut and she heard the latch click inside as Joe had often warned it would.

Chris Beth tried to remember Joe and Wilson's wilderness survival instructions. What would work with rain and snowstorms would work under these conditions—if she could just remember. Wind and hills could distort perception, but imagination was the worst offender. Keep calm. And look for protection. Branches would help, Wilson had stressed. Blindly she felt for the trees. But when she tried to reach for limbs, they were elusive. She felt on the ground and was able to find twigs enough to shield her face so that she dared risk opening her eyes to get her bearings.

Then, making the worst mistake of all, Chris Beth staggered forward only to be driven back by a new horde of insects. When she tried to retrace her steps, the mill seemed to have disappeared. Completely disoriented, she pressed against the force of the winged creatures.

How long she wandered or how far, Chris Beth had no idea. Her last coherent thoughts were a series of questions: *How far am I from home? Did I close the windows of the cabin? Where is young Wil? Where's Vangie? Dear God, who is looking after the babies?* It was almost a relief to feel herself sink weakly and senselessly into Graveyard Creek's shallows even though she couldn't remember if she was upstream or downstream from home.

Stifling the urge to scream, she sat down in the water. Curling up, she thought foolishly that she would just wait until the creatures flew away.

It must have been only minutes, but it seemed like days, before her numb body felt a cold, wet nose on her arm. A wolf? Bear? Did it matter? And then, as if in a dream, she heard a familiar voice, "Esau, good boy! You found my mother!"

21

Where Two or Three
Are Gathered

Still dazed, Chris Beth looked about her. Gradually her eyes focused and she was able to recognize the familiar settees beside the native-rock fireplace of the Norths' Big House.

"Me and Esau just about dragged you all the way," young Wil said proudly at her side. "I mean, Esau and *I.*"

Chris Beth tried to manage a smile. Bits and pieces of the preceding events flashed before her eyes but refused to stay in place. Just as she was able to arrange them into a pattern they fell apart, like a tilted kaleidoscope, and a whole new design emerged. "I'm so confused," she said weakly.

Young Wil was suddenly in control. "You didn't *act* confused," he defended. "You did everything right. Most folks—'specially women—would've been screaming and tearing through the forest. But you—you just stayed put, like a fawn hid out."

Waiting was smart, he said. (*But I had no choice. I was lost!*)

And getting in the water was good. Lots of people had survived "fire and stuff" that way. (*My being there was by accident!*)

"Uncle Wil will be proud of you, M-Miss—I mean, Chrissy."

At the faltering speech, another vague memory-pattern shaped in her mind. Grasshoppers. Near-panic. Being lost. The dog's friendly nose. But something else...*Mother!* That was it—young Wil had called her "Mother."

Maybe the child had been disturbed at the men's leaving him. Or maybe their going to Portland reminded him that his mother had lived there. *More likely,* she thought, *he's in need of affection.*

Impulsively she reached out and drew the small figure close. Well, he was *indeed* a man! A "growing boy" would have pulled away to prove his independence to her and to himself. But young Wil gave her a quick embrace instead. It was a warm and wonderful moment for Chris Beth. The look on the small face, so like his Uncle Wil's, said, "I needed that!"

"Am I a mess?" Chris Beth asked as young Wil straightened quickly.

Vangie! Chris Beth forced herself up from the couch. "Is Vangie all right? And the babies?"

"True and little Mart slept through it all while Vangie took care of shutting up the house—that's why it's so dark. Not from the hoppers. They're gone. Some died and the rest flew somewhere else."

Vangie came in. And, even though her eyes were shadowed with fatigue, she set to work on what must have been a thousand cuts, stings, and bruises. Chris Beth allowed herself to be daubed all over with camphor, but refused the peach-tree-leaf poultice. "Nonsense! There's too much that needs doing. I'm almost afraid to ask about the damages. Bad?"

Yes, the damages were bad. Very bad. Vangie and young Wil tried to describe the situation, often interrupting each other, their words tumbling over each other in their excitement. Surely they must be exaggerating just a little. But no! When Chris Beth looked out the window, she realized that what they told her had been understated, if anything.

To her horror, she first saw that every clapboard of the beautiful white house was obscured in a jellylike mass created by the millions of insects which must have swarmed blindly against the building. Thank goodness for Vangie's foresight in closing the windows, or the inside of the house would be in the same shape!

Fascinated, Chris Beth's eyes fastened on the washpot and the tubs of rinsewater. All were topped with thick layers of dead grasshoppers. She could feel no remorse at their demise. She hoped instead that the creeks and rivers were rising to the flood stage with the huge, evil-looking skeletons. They could flood the Pacific Ocean for all she cared!

Then, when she looked at the three-year-old orchard—which only recently had bloomed like the Promised Land—Chris Beth felt a kind of panic that was worse than what she had experienced when caught in the blinding swarms of grasshoppers—for the beautiful orchard was stripped of all its fruit before the summer sun could color a single one. It was stripped of every vestige of bud, leaf, and new-growth limb. Only bare branches reached out pitifully as if begging the one small, unpromising cloud to bring rain to drown the ugly memories. Oh, how awful!

Numbly Chris Beth looked at the ruins about them. Another setback. Another broken dream. Another reason why they undoubtedly would have to move from here...if there was anywhere left that the demons hadn't attacked....

"The older trees?" Chris Beth asked through stiff lips.

"Ask this young man," Vangie said. "He saved some of the fruit."

"It wasn't much." But there was pride in young Wil's voice. "I just did what the books say to do when trees need protecting from the migrating birds."

"Which is?" Chris Beth encouraged.

"Drape 'em in muslin cloth." She nodded, remembering the gauzy fabric of the Muslin City people. "We use it for straining cider sometimes. Uncle Wil had some on the back porch."

Young Wil followed her gaze to the gnarled apple trees, misshapen with age but still bearing, and the peach trees, which were at their prime of life. The boy somehow had managed to wind the thin material around the limbs of several trees. These trees had blossomed heavily, giving promise of what O'Higgin had predicted to be the most bountiful harvest yet. Now they stood like mummies with little to offer the settlers or the bees. It was unbelievable.

Studying her face, young Wil spoke uncertainly. "I told you it wasn't much."

"Anything is *much* at this point," Chris Beth assured him. "What you did was very brave and thoughtful—something Vangie and I wouldn't have known to do."

He brightened. "I didn't have much time. When you didn't come back we had to find you. But I beat the grasshoppers down off some of the branches. Got the leaves for poultices and stripped off some green apples to bake. Not much," he hesitated, then continued, "but the Bible says, 'Where two or three are gathered in His name—' "

Chris Beth forced a tight smile at the interpretation.

"Well, the second plague *was* a real prophecy, wasn't it?" Chris Beth mused.

Vangie moaned in agreement. But young Wil replied, winking at Chris Beth, "Yes—but the sky *didn't* fall!"

22

Homecoming

The rest of the week passed quickly. Chris Beth, Vangie, and young Wil worked long hours to clean away as many of the invading grasshoppers' signs as possible. It was indeed a hateful task and a most depressing one. Every day brought new revelations of the damages the insects had done.

"They left nothing in the garden but weeds," Vangie moaned, holding a hand to support her obviously aching back.

"And the stink!" young Wil added, holding his nose. He had been raking and burying the remains for days, but still the stench remained. The chickens, having eaten their fill, had lost interest and wandered around to find shade. They would miss the giant-leafed sunflowers, which had been stripped of their foliage and promising heads by the hungry insects in their migratory flight. Only dying stalks were left.

Chris Beth paused on the upper rung of Wilson's pruning ladder. Her arms ached from scrubbing the higher sections of the Big House's once-white siding.

"I've heard that these creatures follow a narrow path. Do you suppose the rest of the valley escaped?"

The others hoped so. They resumed their respective chores. And, even though Chris Beth felt that she could not move even one more muscle, she doubled and redoubled her efforts, doggedly determined to somehow make this a nice homecoming for the men.

"I'll soak for hours, then put on the white blouse you like—maybe let my hair hang down, even bite the stem of the rose from my hat! All to please *you*, Joe. *All to show*

how much I love you...miss you..and need you!"

It was true. She had missed Joe more than she had thought possible, she reflected, as she pushed scrub brushes back and forth. Her hands were red and raw, her nails broken to the quick. Maybe, she thought as she paused to removed a long splinter from her left hand, old Jonas was right.

"Oughta pray for adversity," the circuit rider had declared just before pronouncing Joe and Chris Beth man and wife. "Strengthens the innards and sets th' heart in tickin' order."

But that thought was kind of hard to go along with. Yet Joe's absence had given her a chance to "set her heart in ticking order"! Compared to life with Joe, the past was nothing. Nothing at all. Smiling she worked on.

When the pain in her arms and legs became almost unbearable, she whispered her never-changing, simple prayer: "Carry me just a little further, Lord," she implored. Then, strengthened, she worked on.

Why on earth, then, did she simply crumple up like a rag doll when she finally fell into Joe's arms? And why did she cry now that it was all over?

Reckon the Lord carried me as far as He thought He ought to, she thought through a maze of relief and happiness at seeing the men safely home.

"Sh-h-h-h, sh-h, sh-h," Joe whispered, holding her close to his warm, familiar body while stroking her hair. Chris Beth was glad she had stayed up far too late the night before to bathe and shampoo. Every last detail had to be right. And she could tell from the heavy pounding of her husband's heart that her efforts were not lost upon him.

But he would never know what a struggle it had been. His next statement proved that: "Let me look at you!" Then, holding her off a short distance, he added, "Well, you look none the worse than when I left you—but maybe the pesky hoppers missed these parts."

Of all the—then, suddenly, it was funny! She glanced at her sister, whose blue eyes above the circle of Wilson's arms caught her own. Vangie rolled her eyes heavenward, signaling Mrs. Malone's usual comment, *"Men!"*

23

News from the Big City

"Maybe I over-egged the pudding," Chris Beth recounted to Mrs. Malone later. Certainly her feverish binding up of the wounds left by the life-sucking insects had misled the two men. Joe and Wilson were totally unprepared for the devastation, even as she, Chris Beth, and young Wil were unprepared for the news that the entire settlement had suffered equal loss.

"Wheat crop's completely destroyed—all the gardens and fruit. Not a peach, apple, pear, *anything* left."

"There's *some*," young Wil said stoutly. It was hard to tell who was the prouder of the two, the boy himself or his uncle.

"Any reason why we can't celebrate with green apples?" Wilson asked with the characteristic twinkle in his eyes.

"You'll get a bellyache!" young Wil giggled.

"If so, there's a doctor in the house. Bring me the salt."

Chris Beth relaxed for the first time in days. There was a lot to be talked about and settled. But for now she could see that they were heading for one of those family confabulations that drew them even closer together in times of stress. She offered a silent prayer of thanksgiving. All of them needed this moment.

"What're we celebrating?" Young Wil's eyes danced in anticipation of praise.

His uncle pretended to think. "Well, now, it sounds to me like my nephew's reaching the age of accountability."

The boy stood soldierly tall.

"Then—" Wilson scratched his head as if to revive his memory. "What else was it, Joe?"

"Let's see," Joe played along. "Had to do with books. Oh, I know—the Sears catalogue!"

Vangie let out a squeal. "Did you bring one, Wilson? I mean, did you *really?*"

Young Wil did not wait for an answer. He dived into the saddlebags, bringing out the coveted mail-order catalogue and a sack of peppermint sticks—also knocking over a square package in his rush.

"Whoopee! Enough for everybody to have one—or—" he paused, "five for me?" He licked his lips as the scent of peppermint filled the air.

"Both, if you'll take time to count. And you can hand the package to the ladies."

Together Chris Beth and Vangie ripped off the wrappings, with young Wil getting in the way in an effort to see the contents. "K-A-L-S-O-M-I-N-E," he spelled. "What's that?"

"A new kind of paint for the cabinets," Joe told him. "Sort of like whitewash, only there's tint to be mixed in with the water."

" 'Jersey Cream Color,' " Vangie read. "Oh, how wonderful! Just matches the ruffles on my curtains. Too bad, Chrissy."

" 'Too bad,' she says! Why everybody knows the kalsomine will be the exact shade of the yellow 'Gingham Cat' appliques on mine!"

"Ladies, *ladies!*" Wilson implored. "I suggest to you as I suggested to this young man that there's enough for both, if you'll measure. Now, we're hungry. Does anybody care?"

Vangie sliced the coffee cake she had been saving for just such an occasion. Chris Beth put the coffeepot on to boil. Then both of them ran to sit at the feet of their men and demand that they tell everything—absolutely *everything*— they had seen and heard in the big city. As they listened, Chris Beth determined to savor this time together and put both the past and the future in the Lord's hands, where they belonged.

Portland was big and bustling, the men reported. And awfully dusty. Still rough, though. Rutted by wagon wheels. Lots of potholes from horses' hooves in the winter mud.

Those were city streets? Chris Beth had pictured their being somewhat like the cobblestone streets of Boston or at least the hard-packed streets and roads of her Southern home. No, she was on the wild frontier now, they reminded her, and went on to tell about the "pinchers."

Pinchers! They didn't go in *there?* She shuddered, remembering the stories whispered behind fans about "women of the night" who pretended to be dancers but—well, behaved unseemly. And the men—

But these pinchers were of a different nature. Businessmen of another sort. Carried pouches and—

Oh, chewed *tobacco,* Vangie guessed.

Wrong again. These were men making purchases by measuring a "pinch" of gold dust from a pouch with the thumb and two fingers. Gold, lots of gold. More women now, too. Men could mail-order wives. And (hurrying past that subject), there were ferries most of the way now—well-worth the charge of 12 cents per unloaded horse.

Churches? Yes, several new ones. Rumor had it that the "fair sex" divided their time between "bustin' up" the spirits barrels and going into the gambling halls for church donations.

Scandalous! Did they *really?* And would the men allow it?

That's how they collected. The men were in such a hurry to be rid of the good women that they handed over the day's take.

But now were they ready for the *real* news? "Tell us," Vangie begged.

"Now!" Chris Beth ordered.

Young Wil tried a conspiracy. "Whisper it in my ear," he teased.

"Well, for one thing, the *Eagle* is navigating the Rogue River. And the *Swan*—steamboat, remember?—made it up the Umpqua River." Wilson paused, obviously enjoying himself.

"Yes, yes? Go *on!*" Vangie pleaded. "Are waterways coming closer?"

"The *Lady Oregon* is steaming up and down the Columbia to deliver supplies, pick up mail, and carry passengers."

Excitement mounted as Joe took over to tell of the progress on the railroads. Rails would reach from San Francisco to Portland. "And the first people to be put to work will be our own Chinese families, although talk has it that 4000 more are on the way!"

"Do you mean they beget that fast?" Young Wil's eyes were roguish. His uncle shushed him with a look.

"The newcomers are immigrants," Joe smiled. "A lot will settle here, since tracks are to extend a hundred or so miles south of Portland."

The talk went on for hours. "I'll reheat the coffee," Chris Beth said, although reluctant to miss a word.

"Not until you hear the best!" Joe detained her with a hand. "Wilson has news." She sat down again and waited breathlessly.

But Wilson evaded whatever Joe referred to. "About the stage?"

Chris Beth breathed a prayer. Oh, she hoped for the stagecoach to come through! Most of all, she hoped for that!

"It's coming, all right—" he raised his voice above their squeals of joy, "which means that Turn-Around Inn is in for big business!"

How wonderful, how wonderful! But even in her excitement, Chris Beth found herself thinking, "Now where will we worship come winter and bad weather?" But that too was in the Lord's hands. She returned to her listening...

Young Wil, taking advantage of his new role, finally interrupted the conversation. "I'll start the chores." True and little Mart reminded their parents with lusty lungs that somebody had lost track of time. So, guiltily, the adults sprang to their feet.

Later, back home in their cabin, Chris Beth went over the events of the day in her mind as she tucked the baby into his cradle for the night. She and Joe had to talk, she decided, even though she ached with fatigue from the recent nightmare and she knew he must be exhausted from the long trip. Still, she had to know what the men had found out as a result of their journey. Pleasant as the homecoming had been, and interesting though their reports had been, she realized that they had left the main questions unanswered.

24

To Mend a Broken Dream

Chris Beth snuggled gratefully against her husband's warm body. She wished with all her heart that all women everywhere knew the warmth and security that the love of a good husband provided. Why, the love of a good man was second only to the love of God! If all marriages were like this, then there would be no quibbling, and maybe, eventually, no wars...

She struggled against sleep, but in spite of herself her eyelids drooped. In an effort to stay awake, she tried to elbow herself to a sitting position. Joe immediately eased her back into the circle of his arms and tightened his grip around her protectively. "You rest," she heard whispered drowsily in her hair.

The warm bath she had prepared served to further relax his body—instead of reviving it, the way she had hoped. She drew back just enough to look at the strong, rugged jawline of her husband's face. The light of a near-full moon outlined the high, aristocratic cheekbones. A sculptor's dream, she thought. But the kind, understanding eyes were closed. Maybe what she needed to know could wait... No, she must have reassurance from that sensitive mouth.

"Stop studying my face." Joe's words came so suddenly in the stillness that Chris Beth jumped. Both of them laughed, then he continued, "Unless you want to get kissed?"

Joe drew her close again and claimed her lips with a soft, gentle kiss. Her senses reeled a little, as they always did when he kissed her. *Please, Lord, let it always be like this,* she prayed inwardly.

"If you're wondering if I missed you, my love, that should answer your question!"

"I guess I did want to hear you say it," she admitted, "but that isn't what I was wondering about—" Her voice trailed off, for she was reluctant to break this spell or to postpone his need of rest. *Just one question*, she promised herself. All else could wait for a more opportune time.

"About what?"

"Joe," she burst out, "did you find out anything—I mean about the need of a minister up there?"

He inhaled deeply. "Oh, there's a need, a crying need, Chrissy. I'll tell you about the vigilantes and the fear on both sides—I'll explain everything later. It's nothing we can resolve in a single question-and-answer talk."

Neither the fact that Joe had closed his eyes again nor that she had planned just one question could hold back another. "Do you think one of the churches will call you?"

"More than one, I think. And, by the way, Wilson had encouragement on his book—" His voice trailed off.

"That's wonderful! But, oh, Joe, what happens if our dream here gets broken?"

"We mend it," he said in sleep-softened tones, "with prayer."

Joe's last words were no more than spoken when his even breathing told her he had entered the private world of slumber. Without her! She should be glad he could sleep. Should be, but wasn't. A little resentfully she reached for her cotton wrapper and padded barefoot into the kitchen. She decided against lighting a candle—better conserve every match—and the embers had died in the grate. She moved in the darkness, thinking that it fit her mood, and poured herself a glass of milk. Then she sat down at the small table to think.

"If Joe knows more, why doesn't he tell me?" she whispered to the quiet around her. "I'm his wife!"

Did she imagine the voice that said out of the stillness, "But there's a part of him that belongs to God alone"?

Well, she had no quarrel with that, did she? Rinsing the glass quietly, Chris Beth felt the familiar uneasiness churn within her. Maybe all ministers' wives felt this inner conflict—this need for a certain security they never could have...loving God...wanting their husbands to serve Him... but feeling shut out.

"Oh, Lord, forgive me," she murmured. "I know he loves us both. But how can I help when I don't understand?"

No satisfying answer came, but there was a kind of peace as Chris Beth snuggled against Joe's back a few minutes later.

I'll simply have to resign myself to a different life. Different from back home. Different from other women's lives. Joe has to put God first...and sometimes bear other people's burdens before mine...and I have to understand...maybe that's how dreams are mended....

She drifted off to sleep without a clear resolution.

25

The Burial

Strain showed on every face at Sunday morning's service. Even O'Higgin's song was less lusty, his voice more subdued. *If I'd walked into a group wearing faces like these, I would have gone right back home,* Chris Beth found herself thinking. Instead she had found loving countenances, smiles, and words of encouragement.

"How do you do it all?" she remembered asking Mollie Malone, thinking of what the older woman had gone through caring for her late husband's seven children, the death of one, and all the other hardships—alone.

"Love strengthens the arms," the unflappable Mrs. Malone had said matter-of-factly, "so we can hold each other up."

Remembering that now, Chris Beth felt her own arms—and her heart as well—grow stronger. These people held her up when her legs were limber. Maybe it was her turn now. She felt a surge of strength and joy such as she had never known. It would help Joe to know.

If she could catch his eyes where he stood talking with a group of somber-faced settlers, she would signal for him to give her a minute before going to the front of the arbor. But there was no opportunity. He was moving forward and the others followed. Strange, wasn't it, that they always seemed separated by persons or things just when she wanted to stand by his side?

But Joe needed no help. He had spent long hours on his sermon for today. Still, she was sure that his notes were untouched. Instead, he had taken his inspiration from the congregation. No, the *needs* of the congregation. The inspiration could have come only from the Lord!

111

"We're going to have a burial," Joe announced without his usual preliminaries. The announcement brought dead silence. Chris Beth was as surprised as the rest of the crowd. "Buryin'" meant a funeral and death that they didn't need on top of all the rest of the week's losses.

"Beforehand, I'm going to ask that each of you share your concerns and problems, no matter what their nature. Just talking about our burdens lightens the load."

Brother Joseph was admittedly a special breed of preacher. "Horse of a different color," so to speak. "Kind of a maverick," cattle raisers said. "Never knowed 'im to preach a no-account sermon even on a empty stomach," Nate Goldsmith had declared on occasion. *Still and all,* the school board president's look said, *today could be an exception. Could be,* those who caught Nate's eye agreed.

Seeing the telltale looks, Chris Beth felt a quickening of her own pulse. These people needed help. But it was for her husband that she prayed. Her prayers were so fervent that she failed to hear the faint words from the far front of the arbor at first.

When his voice strengthened, Chris Beth recognized the speaker as one of the Muslin City men. "But we don't ask a handout, just a hand in felling logs afore the rains set in on the ledge."

Now there was a real problem, she found herself thinking. Here they had met to pray for rain while the newcomers were praying that the floodgates of heaven remain closed until they could erect their cabins for protecting their families.

Abe Solomon, usually so retiring, stood to say, "We're havin' real trouble at the store. Folks needin' credit. And supplies hard to come by." Mrs. Solomon affirmed every word with a birdlike bob of her head.

One by one the other men stood. Folks need rain, they said, or the valley would be turned into a desert. There was likely to be a real shortage of food, what with the drought and then the plague. No rain could spell fire, like many years before—and maybe diseases too. The people sure needed a doctor, a real "live-in one," they said pointedly. Even two doctors, or at least a helping hand, like a nurse.

'Course, with no crops now, where was money to be had to pay 'em?

"We need more'n doctors and preachers, too. What're all these young'uns gonna do without dedicated teachers?" There was grave concern in Nate Goldsmith's voice. "Education's our best investment—better'n roads and full stomachs."

A murmur of agreement passed through the audience. The crowd was getting worked up. Women fanned themselves with their bonnets. Some of the men unbuttoned their starched collars. And voices rose to a crescendo. There was no panic, just strong emotion. *These people share their worries like they share all else,* Chris Beth thought—*their joys, their sorrows, each glory of a victory won, each agony of defeat.* Even as she suffered with them, her own heart warmed at the thought. *These are my people! Mine and Joe's...Wilson's and Vangie's...*

Mr. Beltran spoke then. "People are like sheep," he said haltingly, "lost without a shepherd." He paused, then continued more certainly, "We need a shepherd! We Basque folks know how bad we need one—or two—" He looked over the group, "Or more!"

The man's appeal was the first to draw an "Amen!" from what sounded like the entire congregation. Even the cattlemen, who ordinarily treated "woolly raisers" as "trash," added their voices.

When Brother Amos rose, the crowd fell silent. *Not another plague,* their eyes begged. But his words were to reaffirm Mr. Beltran's plea (so obviously aimed, the crowd knew, at the Craigs and the Norths). "Would that Jehovah speak again to those He has called. And this time a mite louder!"

O'Higgin broke in. "Sure'n ye be right," he said. "We be needin' them that can counteract the demons o' darkness—like them dratted hoppers. Regular devil's helpers, they are. And so're the worries that be plaguin' ye all!"

Silence fell over the group. Chris Beth wondered how her husband would respond. She did not have to wonder long. Sensing that the timing was right, Joe began to speak quietly.

"Thank you, one and all." His words were gentle, with humility. "How good to come to the house of the Lord and share our problems. It must warm the Master's heart that the concerns here today are for the good of us all. Not one has brought a personal problem, though I know that every household represented has its share."

Joe waited until the ripple of agreement made the rounds. "Now," he spoke in a louder voice, "it is time to get on with the burial!"

Beneath the arbor, every eye focused on Brother Joseph. Men stopped fingering their wilting collars. Women laid down their fans. Even the feeble breeze stopped toying with the dry leaves overhead. The worshipers outside, who had raised their umbrellas against the sun's merciless rays, strained forward to hear his words.

"I will ask young Wil—may I call him our junior deacon?—to unleash the canoe by the creek. Then, before the rest of the ceremony, let's examine the Scriptures together, praying for the inspiration of the Holy Spirit. Jesus tells us that no man can serve two masters. I ask you then to consider O'Higgin's words. Are we going to be enslaved by our worries, which are forged in the devil's furnaces? Or freed of them by the only Master who can wash away our sins?"

Fascinated, the settlers waited as Joe opened his Bible. In the moment it took for him to locate his text, the curtain lifted in Chris Beth's mind again without warning. The crowds...the longing...the reaching...and the four of them, God's "called people," standing in the center for one wonderful moment. Then the vision faded, but this time it left no dizziness. This time it left no confusion. For this time she knew with a spiritual kind of knowing that her "Why, Lord?" questions to the significance of the phenomena were about to be revealed!

Raptly she listened, along with the settlers around her, as Joe read from Matthew:

> "Therefore I say unto you, Take no thought of your life, what ye shall eat, or what ye shall drink; nor yet for your body, what ye shall put on. Is not the life more than meat, and the body than raiment? Behold the

> fowls of the air: for they sow not, neither do they reap, nor gather into barns; yet your heavenly Father feedeth them. Are ye not much better than they? Which of you by taking thought can add one cubit unto his stature? And why take ye thought for raiment? Consider the lilies of the field, how they grow; they toil not, neither do they spin; yet I say unto you, that even Solomon in all his glory was not arrayed like one of these."

Joe paused and looked directly into Chris Beth's eyes. She nodded, wondering if her face revealed a certain transfiguration of her heart.

Joe read on, his voice rising with new confidence:

> "Wherefore, take no thought, saying, What shall we eat? or, What shall we drink? or, Wherewithal shall we be clothed?...For your heavenly Father knoweth that ye have need of all these things. But seek ye first the kingdom of God, and his righteousness; and all these things shall be added unto you."

Joe's voice slowed deliberately. And as he concluded, his eyes sought and held the enraptured gaze of each member of the group.

> "Take therefore no thought for the morrow; for the morrow shall take thought for the things of itself. Sufficient unto the day is the evil thereof."

Joe raised both hands in supplication and closed the Bible. The crowd seemed to exhale gently in unison. Still, they waited, as if knowing—as Chris Beth knew—that a very dramatic moment was near at hand.

With hands still uplifted and facing his audience, Joe spoke with a forcefulness that none of them had heard him use before. "And so it is that this day we will rid ourselves of the burdens which are barriers between us and the true glory of God—these worries which are tormenting us, twisting our very souls, and robbing us of our visions and dreams!"

Lowering his hands, Joe looked away from the faces in the crowd, his eyes traveling to the banks of the creek, where young Wil stood at attention. The others followed his gaze.

"The boat is ready," he announced to the expectant crowd. "If you will, follow me in person—or at least in your prayers—to the edge of the water."

A little murmur ran through the crowd. Then the group fell silent as, with a purposeful stride, Joe walked toward the little craft. Abe and Nate were the first to respond by stepping behind Joe. Their wives followed. Chris Beth fell in step with Mrs. Malone, aware that the others were close behind. So far, so good. But what on earth did her husband have in mind? She wondered as they walked silently.

At the water's edge, Joe turned to the mystified crowd: "I'll row out to the parting of the current. And there I will deposit these worries of ours, these demons of darkness! We will send them down the creek to the river—and from there to where the river joins the ocean. There they will be buried at sea!"

Joe picked up an oar. Chris Beth knew a panicky moment as he stepped partway into the rocking boat. She wondered if he knew how to row. They had never talked about it. The current was swift out there, but with surprising expertise, young Wil righted the canoe, gave it a shove with the other oar, and somehow managed to leap in beside Joe.

A shout rose from the worshipers standing on the bank of the creek. Joe's face gave no sign of whether he expected it. Maybe he didn't hear. His eyes were closed against the sun and his lips moved as if in prayer.

"Best we be raisin' praise, it is!" O'Higgin boomed. "What song be your choice?"

"Shall We Gather at the River?" the crowd chorused. Seeming to respond to some inner voice, they linked arms then. Their bodies swayed like the ripples on the water's surface. Their voices joined its song.

Chris Beth was too overcome to join in. She clung tightly to the solid comfort of Mrs. Malone's arm on her right and Vangie's on her left, as if she doubted the laws of gravity. But there was a silent song in her heart.

"So *that's* what You and he had in mind, Lord!" she whispered.

26

United We Stand!

There had never been such a sermon preached in this valley before. At least, not that the valley folks could recall. It was sort of like the Bible-poundin' Noah stories. Grandma Pritchett claimed to have known the circuit rider well, but she was given to rememberin' some things that never happened, they said. Maybe he wasn't as all-powerful as Grandma made out. Even *he* couldn't have brought such a varied congregation together the way Brother Joseph did.

"I reckon they'll be stayin'," Nate Goldsmith said.

"Surely, surely," everybody nodded, there being no doubt that *they* meant the Craigs and the Norths. Not that they out and out promised. Best nail down a contract. Speaking of which, something better be done about a teacher.

"Hear that?" Mrs. Malone whispered, giving the tablecloth a popping shake to rid it of dinner crumbs.

Chris Beth moved toward the older woman to fold the corners of the cloth together. "I hear!" she whispered.

"Humph! Year of the Grasshopper, indeed! This is the Year of Miracles. Take my word for it—'United we stand!'"

Almost overcome with the joy of all that had happened this day, Chris Beth could only nod. Together, she and Mrs. Malone packed up the remains of the Sunday meal for the Muslin City people to take home.

"Team's rarin' to go!" Wilson called.

"So are we!" Vangie called back from where she was talking with some of the most recent wagon-train settlers. Then, beaming, she ran to Chris Beth to whisper, "This will be another of our fine evenings together. But let's you and I ride in back again. I need to talk first.

Joe overheard and nodded. She was glad to see that his eyes promised the talk both of them needed together later. Then the two families, including a very proud "junior deacon," boarded the buggy and the team turned toward home.

"Did you bury some of your feelings at the 'burial' today, Chrissy?" Vangie asked as soon as the turning of the wheels would guarantee privacy.

Chris Beth caught her breath in surprise. "Yes," she said slowly, "I did—I mean, I *think* I did—"

Vangie was studying her face, and the knowledge made her uncomfortable. "What about you, Vangie?" she asked quickly without meeting the probing blue eyes.

But her younger sister was not one to be deterred. "I mean the hate, Chrissy."

"For your father?"

"Him—and *me?*" The voice was small.

"Oh, Darling, I never hated you!"

"Of course you did. And you had every right. If I hadn't—well—done what I did, everything might have worked—"

"And I'd have married Jonathan and lived happily ever after? You know that isn't true, Vangie. He deceived us both." She turned to face Vangie then. "Tell me, did you hate *me?* I stood in the way."

"Hate?" Vangie considered a minute. "No, that's not the word. I envied you. And I was jealous. But that's all gone—even before today it was. I guess I needed today just to count blessings, though. And, yes, I was hoping you could bury the past—bury it completely."

"You know, Vangie," Chris Beth spoke slowly, wondering why her breath felt so shallow, "I think I did—the bad parts, anyway. What remains will be disposed of, I promise!"

Just as soon as I can find a way, she added mentally. She realized then that it was not a new thought. Over and over she had tried to rid herself of the brooch, only to have her plan foiled. Was it possible that deep in some secret closet of her heart she had clung to it? Not out of love or sentimentality, nor for its worth (although she knew it was valuable), but because it was a link that spelled security?

For no reason she could account for, Chris Beth suddenly wanted to cry—not bitterly or sadly, but just to "have a good cry," as Mrs. Malone would have called it. She fished in her bag for a handkerchief.

"What are you doing?" Vangie asked as a jolt of the buggy threw them closer together.

"Burying my past," she sniffed.

"In *there?*"

Suddenly both of them were laughing and crying at the same time, their arms locked about each other in warm embrace. "We should thank Jonathan, Chrissy."

"We should."

"We have so much here because of his—our—folly."

"We have."

"And we won't worry about the future?"

"We won't!"

Oh, I will try, Lord. I will try. Just stay with us—unite us....

27

The Miracle of Decisions

"Mrs. Malone says this is to be the Year of Miracles," Chris Beth said as she and Vangie put away the supper dishes.

Vangie extended her lower lip charmingly to blow at a stray curl clinging to her moist forehead. "The first of which would be a breeze."

"No, that would be the second," Chris Beth said as Vangie turned to hang the dishpan in the closet. "Joe's sermon today was the first—Ouch!"

Joe had entered the kitchen noiselessly and had given her a swat from behind. "Joe," she whispered, "the others!"

"Oh, they know about us!" he whispered back. And, instead of backing away as he usually did in public, her husband imprisoned her in his arms. With her back against his broad chest, Chris Beth was defenseless. "Young Wil's outside—just called us to come see the full moon. And Vangie—well, Wilson's retrieving her from the closet. See for yourself."

There was no need to look. Vangie's giggle told the story.

"The moon, you two!" Chris Beth reminded the two men. She pulled herself from Joe's reluctant arms, gave him a teasing kiss, and said she would check on True and little Mart.

The babies were fine. Chris Beth hurried happily to where the rest of the family she loved so much waited in the bright moonlight.

Young Wil stood to motion her to a cane-bottomed chair. Already the men were deep in conversation. In a matter of seconds, she was aware that another miracle was in progress.

"I guess Doc's gift decided me—and, yes, Vangie knew." Wilson's eyes left Joe's long enough to look into Vangie's face. Chris Beth saw the look of adoration that passed between them. "Probably entered it in her diary, but let me break the news. Much as we wanted you and Chrissy with us, we felt it had to be your decision."

"Uncle Wil's talking about all the instruments and stuff that Doc Dullus had," young Wil said in a little aside to Chris Beth. "First, we tried to buy 'em. Office'll be right here for a while."

Chris Beth gave the small hand a squeeze of appreciation, then listened to Joe's words. "I tried—I honestly did—and I prayed, but I just couldn't do it."

She tensed at his words, but only for a moment. "I found I would never be happy anywhere but here," Joe continued. "I guess some are called to serve no matter where. But the Lord called me here."

Surprisingly, Wilson's voice dropped to a confidential, almost confessional, tone. "I guess He called us all here," he said slowly.

"I guess decisions are kind of a miracle," Vangie said. "Maybe this is the second one, Chrissy."

28

Miracle in the Meadows

The following week Chris Beth fluctuated between ela-tion and despair. She, along with the rest of the family and the entire community, was elated over Joe's sermon and its impact—so elated that Joe, noticing how her feet glided so airily and in such perfect harmony, teased her that the cabin floor seemed unnecessary.

That was true. She had put up with the bare ground of the school long enough to know that a person could live without floors. But food was another matter—food and the money to buy it with. And there were days when a cer-tain despair squeezed hard at her heart, trying hard to rob her of the elation. Saturday was such a day.

In an effort to drive away her gloom, Chris Beth decided to try her hand at a green-apple pie. She knew she shouldn't, but young Wil had begged so hard. And, she reasoned, the fruit he had saved from the grasshoppers would be their last of the season. She was in the midst of cutting the lard into the flour for pastry when Mrs. Malone called from the front door.

"News!" she said.

News from the valley's beloved "Miss Mollie" meant *good* news—so good this time that it would not keep until she could tether the horses. The reins lay on either side of the team as she rushed into the door.

"Go on rollin' out the dough," she said practically. "And me, I'll just be parin' the apples. If," she paused tactfully, "you feel they're gonna take a mite more sugar than's good for a body, try some honey. It'll even mellow the flavor."

Then, wrapping an apron around her ample middle, Mrs.

Malone shifted the scene of the news to the Beltran living room. A miracle, she said, had taken place in the Basque family's countryside....

• • •

Rachel looked up from her spinning. "Supper's nigh heated," she said as the Beltran men and Watch, the giant shepherd dog, came in from the day's work. "You taken the sheep to the high meadow, Rube?"

But Burton answered for his father, "Yes'm."

The family ate in silence. Then, at the close of the simple meal, Ruben Beltran spoke for the first time. "Been thinkin' a prayer mightn't hurt none."

She nodded. "Been thinkin' the same."

Again the boy spoke out, and there was a note of excitement in his voice. "Let me—let me!"

With no show of emotion, his parents nodded.

"The Lord is my *shepherd*; I shall not *want*...He maketh me to lie down beside the still *waters*—and I can't remember the rest, Lord, but I learnt it in school and I kin study it some more. Bless my teacher. *Amen!*"

"Been thinkin' some more." Words came hard for Ruben Beltran. "Caint let minds like them go to waste—Burtie Boy's and hers."

Burtie's eyes sparkled. "Miss Chrissy?"

"The same."

"Hush when your pa speaks." Rachel's words, quietly spoken, carried a note of warning. Her son listened with poorly concealed excitement.

"Think I oughta hep out, Wife?"

Help on the school board or that board of deacons that folks been talkin' about? *Both*, his wife said. Gonna take a lot of thinkin'. *No problem, seein' as how he'd started ahead o' the others*, Rachel assured her husband. Was she feelin' welcome to join up? *'Course!* Not much in the way o' crops, what with the drought and all, but Brother Amos made mention o' usin' God's natural gifts in place of money. *Meanin'?*

"Well, I been thinkin' one such gift's my sheep. 'Nother's my wife."

Burtie's eyes flew open wide. Admonitions forgotten, he burst out, "You not gonna give my mama away! It's right you should sacrifice a sheep, but not my mama! You can't, Pa—"

"Finish your meal."

"My meal's finished."

"So's your talkin'." Ruben turned back to Rachel. "You're good at dyin', cardin', spinnin', and weavin'."

Rachel blushed but surprised her husband by saying, "The best."

• • •

In the kitchen of the Big House, Chris Beth stopped criss-crossing pastry over the top of the green apple pie. "You mean? What *do* you mean?"

Mrs. Malone took off her apron. "I mean Joe made 'em all feel a part of us all—woolly raisers or not. I mean Rube's on his way to see Nate. Figure he and Olga can handle the *Cause!* I mean he took Rachel, too. She's never campaigned before, but this time they're stoppin' at every homestead in the Basque parts, gatherin' support."

Chris Beth felt like a slow-reading child who had spent his last dime on an adult-level book. The impression was of viewing an enormous picture—too beautiful and awe-inspiring to believe until she could examine each detail. Only then would she be able to put it together, and believe what she *thought* she was seeing!

"I've talked too much, as usual," Mrs. Malone said. "Leastwise, too fast." She checked on the team with her eye, then continued, "Started a program they're callin' Shearin' and Sharin' 'mongst the Basque folks. Sheep take less grass and water, you know, to produce fine wool. Rachel's gettin' the women together to teach us all the skills we never should've put aside. All of us can knit, given the yarn she's goin' to donate to the Cause."

The *Cause?* Mrs. Malone capitalized the word with her voice.

Oh, *that!* Should've made that clear the first thing, Mrs. Malone apologized. The Cause was the good Lord. Seemed He spoke to Ruben when Joe conducted the buryin'. And, havin' heard the Word, he was spreadin' it. All the Basque people would "join up" Sunday and be pledgin' their goods towards a salary, sort of. And Mrs. Malone wouldn't be a mite surprised if they put a part in the school coffer.

"Mark my word, you'll be offered a contract."

"Contract! You mean to teach *school?*"

"What else?"

"But—but—I'm married—"

"I should hope so, but Nate's been known t' change his mind, if I recall rightly. This'll be one o' th' times. Mark my word!"

"Oh, Mrs. Malone!" Chris Beth rushed forward to throw her arms around her wonderful friend. "It's too good to be true! It would take care of all our needs. Just when I thought everything was falling apart at the seams!"

"Well, now, the Lord jest always seems to have some surprise up His sleeve. You oughta know that by now." And, with a pat of affection, Mrs. Malone hurried out to where the untethered horses grazed.

Chris Beth watched her friend drive away. Oh, there was so much to tell Joe! Of course, Mrs. Malone could be wrong—no, she wasn't going to let doubts spoil this wonderful day. She would set the table with Joe's mother's best china and light a candle. "Joe," she would say calmly," how would you like to have a guaranteed income so you could—"

Oh, mercy! The pie had boiled over in the oven. Yesterday that would have been a real irritation. Today it was funny. Happily, she pulled it from the smoking oven, noting with relief that it was golden brown from the honey oozing through the upper crust.

Let tomorrow take care of its "evils thereof"! Today's joys were "sufficient unto themselves"!

29

Spread of the Miracle

The miracle spread quickly throughout the valley. For, as Mrs. Malone said, "Love's mighty powerful—only thing I know that no amount o' reasonin' can't keep home!"

News of the Basque contribution reached Willow Grove. Brother Amos took the matter to Brother Benjamin. Then Brother Amos and Brother Benjamin called the rest of the "disciples" together. After a meditative silence, the concensus was twofold.

"Our granaries are filled with last year's harvest," said Brother Amos, with face uplifted as if in prayer; "wouldst Thou have us share with our Christian Brother Joseph that which we would plant next year?"

When he sat, Brother Benjamin stood. "We, having no leader save Brother Joseph, perchance should confess to him that our treasury doth hold a widow's mite of gold—from unnamed sources. Moreover 'twas designated for temple-building. And, our bodies bein' Thy temple, wouldst Thou have us nourish, maintain, and repair the temple of Thy servant and his chosen wife?"

Mutely, each head bobbed consent. "Then," said Brother Amos, "we two shall depart forthwith to so advise our total church body."

Mrs. Malone speculated to Chris Beth at the Fourth of July picnic that Bertie Solomon could be depended on in time of crisis to come through. And crisis or no, a body could depend on her to spread the news. And so it was that Mrs. Solomon had declared to all "payin' customers" that prices would have to be *upped* a mite to "help out, you understand. And them that we have to carry till crops is in best

126

be prepared to square up on time. Else no bonus gift on payday, right, Abe?" Abe guessed so, although the arrangements were obviously news to him.

"But turned out he had some news for her, too," Mrs. Malone laughed. "Abe showed some starch right in front of everybody—just up and said, 'Any staples the Craigs buy'll be wholesale. And that goes fer the Norths likewise, all bein' kinfolks of the Lord!' "

O'Higgin said, "Amen be to that! The Good Book tells us that spreaders o' the Word needn't be burdened down with packin' needed garments and bread. 'Twill be supplied!'"

When the Muslin City people heard, they tuned up their fiddles and played a bit louder. True, they'd hoarded the corn for next year's planting, but wouldn't hominy be more sustaining for empty bellies? Surely the Lord had heard their prayers and given them an opportunity to repay in part the many kindnesses of folks here.

People as far away as Portland heard. Trappers were newsbearers, the settlers agreed. Portlanders would be sending books—passels of 'em—for the bigger school. They would be needin' one, wouldn't they? And just maybe, in case of a fire sale or some such, they'd send a peddler around with reduced goods. The miracle enlarged like the hearts.

30

Sacrifice Sunday

By mid-July the heat was unbearable. The settlers stopped talking about the weather. But today was different. This was Sacrifice Sunday!

Two fat little clouds, looking like cumulous kittens, played tag briefly over the mountain, then enlarged with promise.

"Wouldn't it be something if it rained, today being so special?" Young Wil's face was red above the collar of his Sunday shirt, but his eyes sparkled with excitement.

"Very special," Chris Beth agreed, handing him three-month-old Mart as she climbed from the buggy at Turn-Around Inn.

"I can hold True, too," he said stoutly.

He could hold anything this day, Chris Beth knew. The boy had been too excited to eat or sleep since word came that "Sunday next" was the day decided upon to bring "natural gifts" to the altar. Plans were that the "disciples" would show the settlers how to make a common storehouse of their goods. The Craigs and Norths were to be looked after first. The remains would be distributed equally among the others.

Mrs. Malone opened the door. Chris Beth sniffed in appreciation. Coffee. Rising sourdough. "Irish stew?"

"Sure enough. O'Higgin's had the pot boiling out back since daybreak. Give me the babies, Junior Deacon!"

Young Wil's chest swelled with pride, but his eyes were puzzled. "How did you know? Serving's my gift, I mean?"

"Well, I never!" Mrs. Malone pushed the screen door open wider. "Now, what could be a better gift to offer than your young *self*?"

Chris Beth wanted to tell the boy how proud his uncle would be—how proud she was, too—but the O'Higgin-Malone tribe descended upon them all. Six children, an exuberant dog, and an oversized cat, winding in and out between the feet of the guests, made conversation impossible.

"I get little Mart—please, Miss Mollie!" Lola Ann reached to take the sleeping baby from her stepmother's arms.

Amelia and Harmony shoved each other rudely, each wanting to hold the other baby. True took care of the matter. Awakened, she produced the kind of scream that says nobody's arms would do but Vangie's.

"Mind your manners!" Mrs. Malone reprimanded, and then added more gently, "Don't know what I'd have done without these girls this morning. Took a little doin', bein' ready and all."

"I know," Chris Beth said. "It was thoughtful of you to have us over. You're right, it would have been hot at the arbor."

Mrs. Malone pinched the bosom of her best white blouse between her thumb and forefinger and moved it up and down as if to fan her body. "Hot, yes, and fire danger. The arbor's tinderbox dry."

Chris Beth was aware then of Jimmy John, who was holding the family cat up for her inspection. "Him's growed."

"And so have you!" She scooped the youngest of the O'Higgin-Malone clan of stepchildren up in her arms and cuddled him close.

He wiggled free only long enough to show her three fat fingers, then settled back for his share of her attention. *Three years old*, she marveled. One of these days little Mart would be this size. Then he'd be growing like the other boys who had gone to inspect O'Higgin's stew...Andy, young Wil, Ned. And then he would be ready for a life of his own. What would that life be like? Would he be more of the spirit than of the flesh? Would he help preserve the human race? She could watch, love, and protect. But what else would he need? Companionship, for one thing. Yes, as soon as possible, little Mart must have a brother or sister.

"We'd best hurry along now." *Mrs. Malone must have*

let me dream out my fantasy, Chris Beth realized guiltily. The others would be along any minute, and there was sure to be a crowd.

"I'm sorry. It's just so homey that I like to do my thinking here where I was courted and married. And where little Mart came into the world. Now I'm through dreaming. Put me to work."

Mrs. Malone waved away her offer to help. "Take the baby's things upstairs—oh, here come the Smiths!"

In the upper room, Chris Beth lovingly ran her fingers over the posts of the bed where she had laid her satchel. Here, leaning over sleeping flood victims that she and Joe had comforted, he had proposed. Here she had known that it was God's will that they serve Him in this wild new land—for better or for worse.

As she came down the stairs, Chris Beth saw through the east window of the living room that a large crowd was gathering. Women and children were unloading baskets, as usual, but the men, knotted in a group, paid no attention to their horses. Instead, they pointed at the sky. Some looked hopeful while others shook their heads. Did she imagine it or had a cloud passed over the sun? Oh, she hoped so. Rain would come too late to benefit this year's crops, but there was next year to think about. The river was too low to furnish power for the mill, Wilson had said this morning.

He and Joe had tried to lighten the conversation by saying that at least they could cross without fording in most places. But the water table was so low that the wells were drying up. People in some parts had to haul water for miles, then use it over and over. She wondered fleetingly what Mama would say to using washwater to scrub the floors— after the family had bathed in it. How good that there was a spring in back of the cabin! But, oh, she wished it would rain.

During the service there was thunder. Even Vangie, terrified of storms as she was, leaned over to whisper "Goody!" in Chris Beth's ear. Most of the others called a loud "Amen!" at each clap.

Chris Beth was overcome with emotion during the service. Caught up in the spirit of the meeting, she tried to hang onto every word that was said. But, with her ears tuned to the sounds of what she hoped would be a rainstorm, she was sure she missed a few words.

"Wife and I wanta join up," Ruben Beltran said simply. "Been thinkin' on it some time—wonderin' what we had to offer. Well, here's my wife. Rachel, show 'em your goods—and the rest o' you come on up like you was supposin' to!"

More command than invitation, Ruben's words brought a rewarding response. What appeared to be a dozen couples (men in overalls and women in faded calico dresses and sunbonnets) shyly joined the Beltrans. Joe met them at the fireplace, which Mrs. Malone had improvised into an altar by draping it with her best damask cloth.

Extending his hand, Joe greeted the Basque people. "We welcome you," he said warmly. And Chris Beth thought for sure that her heart would burst with joy when a murmure of "Yes, yes" passed through the crowded room and echoed from group to group standing at the doors.

Led by Brother Amos and Brother Benjamin, the "disciples" marched soundlessly forward. "We could share grain from last year's harvest for thy daily bread."

"And serve as they stewards to count the costs," added Brother Benjamin.

Chris could feel rather than see that most of the worshipers seated around her were weeping. But, as Mrs. Malone would say, " 'Twas a good kind of crying," the kind that cleansed the heart.

The "disciples" marched back like the line of prophets they were. The Solomons waited politely until they were seated, and then went up to face the congregation. "Now, our plan is..." and Abe went on to outline the contributions from the general store—with many an interruption from his wife. To avoid Vangie's probable look of amusement (and lest they both laugh), Chris Beth let her glance slide to her left. And what she saw cut short any desire to smile. Maggie Solomon's green-grape eyes, narrowed like a cat's when watching a helpless fledgling fallen from the nest, were fixed on Vangie. And an attractive young woman (could it be the Mrs. Robbins who claimed to have known the family?) was nodding as if she had made an indentification.

Chris Beth forced herself to concentrate. Nothing was going to spoil this service. It was wrong, if not downright wicked, to entertain unworthy thoughts. She must bury them "at sea."

"—More corn than we know what to do with," one of the men from Muslin City was saying, making it sound true. "Some grape cuttings we brung along the trail takin' root. And apple seeds. Mankind! You never saw so many. We know how to graft 'em, you know." He hesitated, then said slowly, "You been so kind—" His voice broke and he was unable to continue.

More tears. The "good kind." But there was no emotion on the face of Mr. Chu when he padded forward, followed by Wong. Politely the little man bowed. Then, patting his heart, he said, "Theese Jee-sus ees here. No speekee Eeng-*leessh* velle well—one son speekee!"

Wong bowed to his father and then to Joe, who bowed back as if it were his custom. "My fath-er wishes to make gift," the boy said. "We have rice and we know Oriental secret how to make grow the rice. My fath-er will make paddy on island by Missee—Miss—Chrissy's school. 'Twill take not much water—"

Miss Chrissy's school! Chris Beth's heart missed a beat. What on earth would people say to *that*?

She was soon to know! Nate Goldsmith signaled by clearing his throat. Four other men stood. "My helpers, *Mr.* Solomon," Nate emphasized the title, "*Mr.* Beltran, *Mr.* O'Higgin—and this here's the other member of the board. A newcomer. Name's Orin Robbins."

Robbins? Wasn't that the name of the couple who had known her family? Chris Beth supposed that would be Mrs. Robbins beside Maggie...

An earthshaking clap of thunder interrupted her thinking. But the "President" refused to let an act of nature steal his moment of glory. As the thunder rolled on to jolt the surrounding mountain, Nate shouted his announcement. "Your next year's teacher!"

Somebody new—oh, no! The entire audience seemed to in-hale sharply along with Chris Beth. Then the rest happened so quickly that Chris Beth was uncertain which happened first—Vangie's hand squeeze, Wilson's pat on her shoulder, Mrs. Malone's embrace, or Nate Goldsmith practically drag-ging "Miss Chrissy" forward.

That first "Amen!" may have been a response to the thunderbolt. But the rest of them were for their beloved "next year's teacher!" Not that Nate was to be upstaged by an audience, either. "Contract's more liberal—got it right here in my breast pocket. I call on ye all to witness the signin' if'n ye be of a mind."

The crowd would no longer be called to order. Did she know? *Well, not really.* Did "Brother Joseph" know? *Well, maybe—no, not really.* Look at them books! Did she know 'bout them? *Well, sort of.* Was she 'ware that the *legislature* was gonna help? Their questions left Chris Beth no time to think beyond the moment. It was real. The vision was real! She, Joe, Vangie, and Wilson stood in a circle of love.

31

Gathering Storm

There was no rain on Sacrifice Sunday. After blowing themselves up into genielike proportions, the playful thunderheads floated back to sea. Chris Beth's body was filled with vigor in spite of the enervating weather. She cleaned the cabin, pressed and repaired her school clothes, and fussed with her hair. Would bangs be a nice change? Should she do away with the braided crown and maybe do her hair in chignon like she had seen in the mail-order catalogue? Or maybe a pompadour? Maybe Joe would help her decide.

But Joe disappointed her. He was so busy with the new responsibilities of full-time pastor that he seemed unaware of any change in Chris Beth's appearance as she tried the styles one by one. Or was something troubling him? Didn't he want her to teach?

A little piqued at her husband's seeming indifference, Chris Beth had tried to attract his attention several times. "Are you writing your sermons now?" she asked once.

Joe looked startled. "Not exactly. Did you need something?"

Yes, she did! But how does one put it into words?

Then, another time, seeing Joe hitching Dobbin, she said, "If you're calling this afternoon, I'm free. Little Mart and I—"

Joe's answer was too quick and his tone too abrupt. "No! What I mean is, it's business."

Anger, unreasonable though it might be, flared inside her. And, turning away from a probable good-bye kiss, Chris Beth gathered little Mart in her arms and hurried across

134

the foot-log to the Big House. Vangie would understand. Not that she would tell her, of course. But they could talk, stopping just short of what troubled them, and understand. Of course, today might be different. It would feel good to say, "Joe is cutting me out of his life—just when everything should be so perfect!" No, she wouldn't say that—not when her sister had a storybook marriage. Wilson was more open, more expressive, more *ardent*.

With that thought, her face burned. That was a disturbing thought. Chris Beth stopped and, making sure young Wil had not spotted her, stepped behind a tree. What was wrong with her, anyway?

"I'm being unfair to your father," she said to the baby.

Little Mart clutched at the air with both hands. She kissed a fat fist. And, at his coo, she whispered, "I was being disloyal and—maybe *unfaithful*—comparing him to another man."

Back home, Chris Beth took down her pompadour and braided her hair into a crown, then busied herself with Joe's favorite molasses pie. "Maybe," she mused aloud, "something of the old Chris Beth pride sealed my lips." But inside she knew it was more the new-woman love and understanding that changed her course of action.

"Thank You, Lord, for teaching me restraint," she was to pray that evening. For, when Joe came home, he reached out his arms and said, "Ummm, nice—cinnamon! Molasses pie? And I like your hair."

Ashamed, she turned away to hide the tears. Joe didn't notice as he was drawing her to his easy chair. "We must talk," he said.

There, in the circle of his arms, Chris Beth heard a story which explained Joe's preoccupation and drew them closer together than ever before. It was a story which shocked, frightened, and repelled her, and showed her how trivial by comparison her dark imaginings had been. It was a story which portended a storm far greater than any clouds in the sky could threaten, no matter how ominous.

When Joe finished his report, he waited quietly for Chris Beth to react. There was so much to say, and so little! She marveled, as she had so often before, at his sensitivity—

always so silent and so gentle in a time of crisis. And crisis seemed to be her way of life!

"This—this Susanah Robbins told Vangie's whole secret to Maggie?" she asked at last.

"All she knew. Enough for creating an ugly story. Maggie has a way of siphoning information and adding to it. Probably posed as a near and dear friend of yours."

"And Susanah's in need of a friend. But, Joe, what will it do to Vangie if Maggie spreads the story now?"

"She has," he said quietly.

"Did she make Vangie sound like—like a bad woman? How did Maggie know what to ask—I mean, where and who? But, of course," she said slowly, "postmarks, and the name *Stein*—Vangie's use of her maiden name to pass for a recently bereaved widow. But he would have married her—Jonathan would!" She felt herself defending her younger half sister as always, even at her own exposure. "He jilted *me* because of the baby—and True's *not* illegitimate. She's a North!"

Joe held her close. Her storm soon passed. But Vangie's lay ahead....

32

The Plain and Simple Truth

One week passed. Then two. Quickly, time fled in the lives of the Craigs and the Norths—too quickly, Chris Beth felt. They were so busy putting their houses in order that there was little opportunity for their cherished talks. By nature an introspective person, she missed her more leisurely days of being able to think things through. Being the wife of a minister demands its pound of flesh, she admitted in her heart. But even that thought was cut short by a familiar voice.

"They came! You know, the instruments and stuff—they came. Doc Dullus brought 'em!" Young Wil, who had come for Joe to help shift some furniture to the upstairs of the Big House, was panting with excitement.

"Really?" Chris Beth and Joe chorused. She laid aside the schoolbooks she was sorting and Joe stopped sacking the remaining cornmeal he had brought in from the mill. These jobs could wait!

Joining hands, with young Wil leading and Joe following Chris Beth with little Mart in his arms, they formed a human chain. Laughing, they almost skipped across the foot-log, and Chris Beth could have vowed that the baby laughed out loud!

Wilson met them at the front door, outwardly composed. But when he spoke, his voice was unsteady. "Joe, old pal, it's happened. I'm a doctor. These instruments say more at this point than my degree!"

Chris Beth smiled with the others, but her eyes rested on a new wooden plaque on the west wall of the large living room: WILSON JEROME NORTH, M.D. Beneath it hung the sacred Hippocratic oath—second only to his Bible, she knew.

Vangie, who was sewing a button on a white garment, followed her gaze. "That says more than either the instruments *or* the degree to him," she whispered to Chris Beth.

"You, too, I can see—but what are you sewing? I thought you'd be holding a board or something!"

"My nurse's uniform," Vangie said simply. "This will be the reception room. Opens into the library, you know. Closet's for supplies. And there what his parents once planned to be a music room will be used for surgery. Upstairs we may make room someday for overnight patients."

Wilson measured a bureau and laid down his yardstick. "Dream on, Florence Nightingale," he said with a smile of appreciation at Vangie's glow. Then, turning to the others, he added, "But we *will* be needing the room as industry spreads and the settlement grows."

"Undoubtedly," Joe agreed. "And meantime you'll be making house calls like Doc?"

"By mandate of my benefactor—not that I mind. Nice, huh, for me and my angel of mercy? The right instruments. And a live-in nurse!"

Chris Beth studied her sister closely. Flushed with happiness, she looked less tired, but the beautiful planes of her face were too thin and a small blue vein that Chris Beth had never noticed before pulsed along the left temple. Something about the look was disturbing.

"Are you tired out from all this, Vangie?"

"No—well, I guess I am, a little. I'll rest later. For now, everything's perfect. *Everything!*"

Please, Lord, let it stay that way, Chris Beth prayed inwardly. *How good that God hears silent prayer!* she thought. Otherwise He would never hear above the bumping and groaning as the men moved the heavy bureau upstairs.

The workday ended with an omelet supper—no real surprise, since young Wil prepared the meal, and omelets were his specialty. But the meal had a surprise ending—spiced apples from one of the limbs the boy had wrapped against the onslaught of the grasshoppers!

"This is a good omen," Vangie declared. "Now, what would you like for a reward?"

Young Wil looked questioningly at Wilson. At his uncle's nod of consent, he refilled the coffee cups, then took a cup from the china cupboard for himself, filled it with milk, and added a single teaspoonful of coffee.

In such a happy-ever-after atmosphere, how could anybody really believe a fellow human being capable of malicious mischief? But Maggie Solomon, Chris Beth was soon to learn, was doing her homework well.

• • •

August came. The month itself seemed to be gasping for breath. Little dust devils, a sight seldom seen in the usually verdant, grass-woven valley, danced in hot-breathed glee and sucked at the few leaves which the grasshoppers had missed.

"What I wouldn't give for a great big watermelon!" Mrs. Malone said one Sunday at church. "Usually ripe before now."

"And what *I* wouldn't give fer a rain." Mrs. Solomon's voice carried its usual ring of complaint and then a sound of accusation: "We *prayed* fer rain!"

Her husband wiped his face with a red bandanna, measured the distance between himself and Bertie, then wondered, "Did ye set a date?" She flounced away without replying.

That very day, clouds again gathered. Briefly they furnished a relief from the sun. Then, mockingly, they moved over the mountains.

Chris Beth wondered fleetingly if Maggie could be playing the same kind of game—moving in, threatening, and then moving away as if biding her time. Certainly her eyes wore the same mocking expression. She dismissed the thought but decided that she must make a point of introducing herself to Susanah Robbins. She should have done so long ago, but the young woman seemed shy, usually hurrying away as soon as the worship service was over.

Wilson's practice grew rapidly. One of the children on the ledge—no longer Muslin City, as most had cabins now—

broke a collarbone. Lucy Smith gave birth to twins, with her labor made more difficult because of her fear of a doctor, Wilson reported. A midwife had delivered her other two children. Vangie had assisted and had come home vowing that the next addition to the North household would be twins.

Chris Beth cared for True on the days that Wilson made house calls. When the buggy was available, Joe called on newcomers and bereaved families, and it was her turn to leave little Mart with Vangie and accompany her husband.

"Truly," she said to Joe on one such day, "it's all a dream come true."

Joe squeezed her hand, but he looked preoccupied. "Is the heat getting to you badly today? I mean..." he hesitated, "I thought we'd stop by the Robbins' cabin."

"Oh, let's," she agreed. "And I'm fine, Darling—no problem."

The Robbins family, unfortunately, was not at home. A note on the door said "At General Store."

"Just what I'd like to discourage," Joe murmured as if to himself. "Oh, here's Nate."

Nate Goldsmith reined in alongside the Craigs. "Heat's botherin' my gout. Thought I'd best see Wilson. 'Course, could be I'm bilious. Need to see 'im anyway. We're choosin' up rightful deacons, you know. Still and all, there's a matter needin' discussin'." It was hard to tell if the sigh he gave was one of regret or pleasure, Chris Beth thought with amusement. And then his words struck full force.

"Them chose jest hafta meet standards! Like preachers 'n teachers, ya know? And (*ahem!*) him—Doc—Brother Wilson—bein' a doctor 'n all—"

"I'm sure Wilson qualifies," Joe said quietly. "What's troubling you—I mean *really* troubling you, Nate?"

Nate shifted his eyes from Joe's steady gaze. "Well, their families—uh—hafta measure up. Can't have no talk—and talk is—" He stopped as if expecting Joe to understand.

"Yes?"

"Well, we'll be discussin' it come Wednesday noon. Maybe you'll wanta be there too. I mean, you kin tell *him*. Meetin's at my house."

Nate would have wheeled away, but Joe raised his voice, "Stay put, Nate. I think it's wise we leave Wilson out of this for the time being. But, yes, *I* will be there. And I expect you to have the accuser there, too. Understood? Come to think of it," Joe went on slowly, "let's switch the meeting place to the general store. That's where all the talk began, isn't it?"

Clearly the question caught Nate off guard. He flinched under Joe's steady gaze and concentrated on the rear of his mule. "Needs his tail curried. Gen'ral store 'tis then," he muttered in his beard. Obviously anxious to be off, Nate rapped the animal sharply with his cowhide crop. "Giddyup, you sluggard!" He all but shouted and disappeared in a swirl of dust. Chris Beth choked back a sob.

It was all too much. The dust. The heat. Plus the ugly situation and what it might mean to the four of them—particularly Vangie. There was no holding back the tears of frustration. "They're making it all up. I mean, they're adding to it—stacking the evidence—"

"And we'll unstack it." Joe's voice was firm. "We'll tear down their little house of dominoes. But you and I have to talk, Chrissy."

Something in his voice unnerved her. "What about? Oh, Joe," she burst out, "just hold me in your arms!"

He bent and kissed her gently. "Later, Darling—and for the rest of your life! No distractions now, though. We have to finish the conversation before we get home.

Mutely, she nodded.

At Joe's signal, Dobbin moved forward. "Whatever information I have has come piecemeal," Joe said.

"Has it mattered?"

"Ordinarily it wouldn't. You know that. But now it does. I have some ammunition which has nothing to do with you girls. The other will have to come from you."

"What do you want?"

"I want the plain and simple truth."

The truth—plain and simple. Chris Beth bit at her lower lip until she felt the salty taste of blood. *Oh, Joe Darling, don't you know that the truth is seldom plain, and never is it simple?*

She told him then, haltingly at first, then with gathering strength. There would be no more secrets—even little ones—to stand between them. Any remnants of the glacier once inside her heart melted into warm new seas as she talked of Jonathan Blake's proposal...their wedding plans...the broken engagement because of "another woman"...the bitterness when she found her rival was Vangie...and then the heartbreak and humiliation when she found that her half sister was carrying Jonathan's child.

Then, from force of habit, Chris Beth found herself defending Vangie's honor. "She was a child, Joe, a 16-year-old child and very naive. She was overprotected by her mama and disciplined by her father. That's how it all started, you know, with the difference in our names."

"You mean Vangie's having used her maiden name to differ from yours? Yes, I know."

For a short time all was silent except for the sound of the buggy wheels and the rhythmic clop of Dobbin's hooves. At last Joe spoke. "Is there anything else I should know?"

"No—well, do I need tell you that it was Vangie's only mistake? I mean, there had never been anybody else—"

Joe remained silent. What could he be waiting for? Surely he didn't think—oh, no, he *couldn't*! At the thought, Chris Beth felt hot color stain her cheeks.

"Joe—Joe, you don't think—I mean, you know there was nothing irregular between him—Jonathan Blake—and me." Her voice dropped. "There's never been a man in my life—that way—but you—"

Joe halted the buggy. Then deliberately he folded her in his arms as if keeping his promise. Maybe he would never let go of her again! "And I thank you. What a beautiful gift to a man!"

Chris Beth loved her husband as never before. And that was the truth—*plain and simple*!

33

Wednesday at Noon

In the two nights following the encounter with Nate, sleep would not come easily for Chris Beth. She lay wakeful and restless after Joe slept. It was so hot! Even the white rays of the waning moon brought imagined heat through the open windows. But it was not the heat that made her listen to the eerie hooting of the owls in wide-awake fear and fascination. It was dread of the Wednesday noon meeting (*or was it a trial?*).

On Wednesday morning she stole from bed even earlier than usual. The slice of moon had moved behind the western mountains. In the inky blackness she felt her way to the bedroom door and, careful not to latch it, closed it softly behind her. In the kitchen she lighted a lamp and shielded its light from the window lest Joe awaken and advise her to stay at home today. But all precautions failed.

Before she finished braiding her hair, a soft click of the latch told her that Joe had discovered her bare pillow. She felt rather than saw his questioning eyes in the dim lamplight.

"Good morning!" The greeting was bright enough, but her next words sounded insincere even to her own ears.

"I—I need a few things. I mean, I'll look more than buy—get ideas, you know, to see if bustles are in or out. In or out of style, that is."

He looked down at her seated figure a long time before answering. "You are welcome to come along, Chrissy. You know that. But do you think it is wise?"

"I do for a million reasons."

"You need not name them," he answered, turning up the

wick of the lamp. "Now let's get the coffee brewing."

• • •

CENTERVILLE! The sign loomed up as Joe called, "Haw, Dobbins!" and the horse made the ordered left turn for the general store. Before Chris Beth could ask questions, she saw the crowds congregated around the buildings she knew, and the new buildings as well.

"Joe," she gasped, "are they all here for the same purpose—to witness our humiliation?"

"I don't know why they're here, but not that, I'm sure." He hesitated. "Chrissy, are you sure—?"

"Of course I'm sure! I belong by your side no matter what." When his head jerked toward her in surprise, she laughed. "In spirit, I mean. Actually, I will be shopping around."

The few hitching posts were taken. As Joe drove past the buildings in search of a shade tree where Dobbin could rest, Chris Beth had a chance to see just how much development had taken place since her one-time visit...IVERSON'S LUMBER...LIVERY STABLE...FEED & SEED...BIG TIME SALOON... CENTERVILLE HOTEL, *Cheapest in Town & Only One*...CAS-CADE SHIPPING...TOM BURGHER, ASSAYIST...Her eyes smarted from the dust and she was unable to read the other signs. She made a mental note to meet this Tom Burgher. Then, forgetting the mission of the day, Chris Beth felt the old frontier excitement. "It's all happening, isn't it, Joe? The growth's really taking place."

"Yes," Joe said, "it is! And let's hope the growth's heading in the right direction."

"I see what you mean." Some of the hastily built structures housed essential businesses. But with them came the less desirable ones, such as the saloon. And she wondered about the hotel itself, especially the upstairs rooms. She was sure she saw women's faces hidden discretely behind the soiled muslin curtains. No churches, though. And no doctors, as far as she could tell.

As Joe tethered Dobbin beneath an oak tree near the blacksmith shop, more questions rose in her mind. Loud, angry voices came from the direction of the general store.

Where are them sheep the crooked Yankee promised to deliver? Yeah, *yeah!* Purebreds they wuz, too. Good money paid out 'n lost.

Be here in time. Replacements comin'.

Replacements? Fer what? Well, first herd was drowned. Had to float 'em over the Columbia on a raft. Raft upset in the rapids and stupid critters cain't swim. Second herd, kinda hard to explain, but all uv 'em turned out to be males...

Bully fer them! Us cattlemen never wanted them woolies here...

Joe took Chris Beth's arm and guided her firmly toward the store. As they entered the door a shot rang out, followed by the sound of horses galloping away. "Nobody hurt, folks! Come on in!" Abe Solomon motioned from the door.

The smells of camphor, new linsey cloth, liniment, and Kennedy's pills were inviting to the nostrils compared to what was going on outside. Mrs. Solomon was nowhere to be seen, but the pretty, voluptuous Maggie was very much visible! Wearing a low-cut, tight-fitting red dress, the girl moved from one male customer to another so obviously that it was embarrassing. *This woman dared bring charges against Vangie!* Anger filled her body. Then, sickened, she turned away.

"Meetin's in the side room, gents." At Mr. Solomon's announcement, there was stomping of boots mingled with squeaking-new shoes and then the soft padding sound that said Mr. Chu. Chris Beth clenched her hands into tight fists and tried to concentrate on an outdated copy of *Godey's Lady's Book.* "Printed in Boston," she read. How well she knew! Mama used to study the fashions by the hour.

Boston! Where she had met Jonathan...where he had led Vangie astray...the reason for this terrible meeting. No, she must concentrate on the fashions. She opened the book.

"Oh, here's a beauty. Bell-shaped skirt and probably hooped. Wouldn't it be lovely made of the velvet Mama sent last Christmas. Lots of crinoline petticoats, of course—"

Chris Beth was unaware she had spoken aloud until a soft, familiar hand touched her elbow. "It would indeed! And there's enough for both of us."

Vangie!

34

He That Is Without Sin

Confusion followed. Chris Beth and Vangie embraced and clung to each other, too overcome with emotion for words. Somewhere in a part of her mind, too numb to function at the moment, Chris Beth wondered about the babies. But before she could gain control of her thoughts, she and Vangie were surrounded by a pair of motherly arms.

"Mrs. Malone! Where—how—?"

But her words were drowned out as another pair of arms circled the group from the other side. And then another! Faces she knew and loved—all of them drenched with tears—appeared one by one until all the women in the settlement knotted together in the center of the store. Through her own tears, Chris Beth tried to force her eyes to focus and her mind to think clearly.

"How did you all know? Who told you—and why—?"

"Now, does it matter a-tall? Folks always rally 'round in time o' trouble. And if you're wonderin' where the babies are, young Wil's carin' for 'em both. Now, for goodness sake, let's get from under this flypaper. Dollars to doughnuts it's stuck in my hair a'ready!"

After speaking, Mrs. Malone touched her hair experimentally and, finding it free of glue, blew her nose and tried to back away. The others were not to be rushed. Each in turn, with unaccustomed show of emotion, kissed the two girls before joining the outer circle of women, most of whom Chris Beth knew only by sight.

"Now!" Mrs. Malone was her usual practical self. "I suggest we ladies jest kneel right here for a word of silent prayer."

And that is how the men saw them when the door opened quietly to let Mrs. Solomon out of the side room "Musta felt right ashamed," Mrs. Malone was to comment later. *Mrs. Solomon?* "No," she said to Chris Beth, "the men, no less! Bertie come through like I told you she does in time o' trouble—downright told th' men she didn't have much evidence, at that."

But Wednesday noon Chris Beth saw only the woman's whitefaced fury as, with a rustle of starched skirts, she passed the kneeling group without a nod. "You!" Mrs. Solomon hissed from the back of the room, "you go next."

"*Me!*" The voice was unmistakably Maggie's. "I'm not the one who gave birth to a—"

"Mind yer mouth. Yer the one who brung it up. And yer gonna prove it or hold yer tongue ferever. Now *git!*"

Guiltily, Chris Beth realized she was kneeling for prayer and eavesdropping at the same time. "Forgive me, Lord," she whispered, and rose to her feet.

Vangie rose with her. "Watch for Wilson," she whispered. "He's treating the Smith baby's colic. He may try to stop me."

"From what? You don't mean—"

"I mean," Vangie interrupted in a firm voice, "that I'm going in there."

And with that she was gone. As if in a terrible dream, Chris Beth heard the gasp of protest from the men as Vangie followed Maggie into the meeting. At the door, her beautiful baby-sister-grown-tall turned, sent a small and uncertain smile her way, and quietly closed the door.

Some of the women rose. Others, aware of a new crisis, remained on their knees. For how long Chris Beth was unable to determine. She lost all track of time as her surroundings seemed to shimmer and swirl in warning. Again the crowds. The happiness followed by anger. The reaching out to Joe but being unable to reach him. Then someone dragging her—toward Joe? Backward? Or into the future?

"No!" Had she actually cried aloud? Did she imagine the viselike grip on her arms? There could be no doubt as to the reality of the voice.

"Vangie! Where's Vangie?" Wilson demanded, shaking her.

Wordlessly she pointed to the closed door. Immediately Wilson spun on his heel and turned. But when he would have left her, Chris Beth reached out and caught his arm, gripping it as he had gripped her own arms just moments ago.

"Wait! We're all in this together. I'm going with you." Wilson did not object.

At the sight of them there was a long hiss of intaken breath, followed by strained silence. In fear and humiliation, Chris Beth faced the group. Back home, "ladies" did not make such unladylike entrances. And here in the settlement, "womenfolk" did not "meddle in men's affairs." *So what*? She was her father's daughter. She was Joe's wife. And she was a child of God. As such, she claimed rights none of them better dare dispute!

Maybe something in her eyes said as much. The men seemed to exhale as Joe moved to the front of the room where Nate stood. "May I take over?" Actually, the question was more a command. "We are *all* here now. And the rest of you have had your say."

Faces showed no expression. It was hard to tell what had gone on before. Chris Beth observed only that one of the men had given Vangie his chair and that Maggie, white-faced but defiant, stood pressed against the wall near the back of the room.

"Wilson and I have served you all our lives," Joe said quietly. "We intend to go on serving—but we can only serve those who are willing to be served. If, for whatever reason, you find us unworthy, we need to know. But as for this— this tempest in a teapot—I am ashamed, yes, *ashamed* that those responsible would stoop so low!" His voice rose powerfully. "Who is Vangie's accuser?"

When the men turned to look at Maggie, she had the grace to blush. But her eyes were cold and merciless. She looked incapable of remorse. Then, to Chris Beth's horror, she took a step forward.

About midway the girl seemed to hesitate, but defiantly she said, "I am! I'm not afraid of her kind—"

"*Her* kind!" Wilson would have sprung forward except for Chris Beth's restraining hand

"Don't," she whispered. "Please—you'll only make it harder for Vangie!"

Then, mercifully, Joe was speaking in crisp tones. "Let's get on with this at once! You may come on up, Miss Solomon. And you men may feel free to interrogate the witness. But I would remind all of you, and that goes for you, Maggie, to use discretion! In the words of Jesus, let he that is without sin cast the first stone."

Maggie's hips swayed as she walked toward Joe.

Nate stood. "You got any proof, girl? Proof that Doc's missus is less'n she's supposed to be?"

Maggie's laugh was harsh. "What better proof than that b-b—that *child* of hers!" Chris Beth flushed. Why, *child* sounded bad!

Wilson pulled away from Chris Beth's grasp. Joe, seeing the struggle, left the front of the room and hurried to Wilson's side. The men spoke in low tones above the sudden commotion in the room.

"Should be tarred 'n feathered...cheap, no-good woman startin' such commotion from hearsay...and all fer what purpose...now, lest you got more proof than this...say, what's *your* occupation anyways? Be ye without sin?"

Fear clutched Chris Beth's heart. What was all this leading to? What were they accomplishing? *And where was Vangie?*

In her preoccupation with making her way through the group to find her sister, Chris Beth bumped into Maggie Solomon, who was attempting an unexpected getaway. "You haven't heard the last of this," Maggie hissed. "You and your sweet-faced little sister!"

Before Chris Beth could recover from the unprovoked attact, Joe pounded on the table with his gavel. "Let her pass!" His voice carried a command. "Then please remain standing for the benediction: *Father, forgive them, for they know not what they do!*"

35

The Third Plague

' The Centerville incident was history. Only on occasion was it a topic of conversation in the Big House or between Chris Beth and Mrs. Malone.

"Is it all behind you now, Darling?" Chris Beth asked Vangie once as they made soap in the coolest part of the morning.

Vangie's violet eyes widened. "Oh, I put it all behind ages ago," she said innocently. "I just pray the others have. Poor Maggie—"

Chris Beth suspected that Joe and Wilson discussed the matter. Wilson, given more to quick anger than Joe, seemingly held no grudge once matters were settled. And Joe was good at calming him. Their main concern was only that the girls not be humiliated or left with blemishes on their names. Chris Beth and Vangie knew that Wilson had put the incident in its proper perspective when he accepted the deaconship with humble pride and made plans for his and young Wil's ordination.

Mrs. Malone caught Chris Beth up on other outcomes. "Poor Nate— maybe one day he'll learn," she said, shaking her head. "He's a good man—just self-important like. Couldn't a' married a more fittin' wife. You wasn't in the store when Bertie made Maggie apologize?"

"To *Vangie*?"

"No, to the august body of men who'd been beguiled into havin' that silly investigation! They ordered her to stay away from Vangie—said Mag wasn't fit to keep her company."

"That seems harsh, doesn't it? Maggie must feel terrible."

"Maggie never felt terrible in her life—less'n she's ignored by a man. And you know what place has no fury like a woman scorned! Gettin' back t' Nate Goldsmith. His wife said mor'n Maggie was to blame. Marched 'im right in and talked a streak. He'll be apologizin' to the rest—Vangie, you, Joe, and Wilson."

"Oh, but—" Chris Beth started to protest.

"Olga's verdict, not mine. And, child, Nate *did* put you through a heap."

Yes, he did, at that. He and Maggie. But it was past. The Lord had seen them through it. And the hard part now was to pray for a girl like Maggie. But she had learned that enemies are no longer enemies in a true sense when she prayed for them. And certainly the girl needed prayer. She had all but taken up residence at the Big Time Saloon ("*Bed* 'n Board," Mrs. Malone phrased it, emphasizing the *bed* part just enough to convey the message).

But for Vangie and those who loved her so much the nightmare was over.

In the days that followed, Chris noted gratefully that it was business as usual with the valley folk. There were no curious stares and no overeffusiveness. They simply folded the matter away and forgot it as quickly as possible in the same manner they disposed of long underwear after a long, hard winter.

Anyway, there were some pressing matters at hand. Lots of unfinished business. Then the new business, which caught the already weary, emotionally drained settlers completely by surprise.

* * *

"Best we git all things settled," said Nate Goldsmith (acting as president of the board instead of as judge or chairman of the nomination committee for deacons) when he called on Chris Beth the first week in September.

In his hand was the "revised contract" for the coming school year. "Terms bein' much the same as last year—exception bein' this allows fer teacher's bein' married. This meetin' with your approval?"

"I'm sure it's all right—" Chris began, but when she reached for the folded paper, Nate drew it back.

"Wanted t' say it's too bad 'bout the misunderstandin' 'n all. But let bygones be bygones, I allus say?"

Chris Beth nodded soberly at his implied question, smiling inwardly. That was as close to an apology as Nate could come, although his obvious face-saving tactics were amusing. His words *sought* no forgiveness. They gave it!

"Jest sign on the dotted line!" he said, obviously relieved that she did not pursue the "bygones."

Unfolding the paper, she saw that Nate had handed her the old contract. He had simply crossed out her signature and penciled in a line of dots above it. "Make sure you sign your married name!"

"Making sure," she said.

In mid-September, the new board of deacons met to decide how to proceed with erecting some sort of storehouse. The "disciples" met with them, and Brother Amos brought a plan he had sketched. "Art thou willing to consider a silo contructed of split rails?"

Wilson and young Wil brought the sketch home and excitedly shared it with Joe, Chris Beth, and Vangie. "Looks practical," Joe decided. "Did hands volunteer to help?"

"All present," Wilson said. "And word will spread."

"How much money's involved?" Joe's brows knitted in concern.

Young Wil could keep silent no longer. "None! That's the good part. Abe—I mean Mr. Solomon—is furnishin' nails an' stuff."

A week later the school board met to decide which the community should devote its energies to first—the storehouse or enlarging the school. Unanimously they decided to tackle both! "Been thinkin'. They's 'nuf uv us now t' do the Lord's labor," said Ruben Beltran.

Then the following Sunday O'Higgin announced that the deacons thought a choir might be nice. "Be ye of th' same mind?"

The congregation responded with loud hand clapping. "Then I be th' leader and Miss Chrissy there, will ye be soloist, me bonnie lass?"

Again, the clapping. "I will be happy to!" Chris Beth answered, feeling tears of joy near the surface. Finding time to do all the responsibilities she was assuming would be a problem. But, like Mrs. Malone said, "A body always ends up doin' what he calculated bein' important!" Well, singing again—and this time for the Lord—was important. And it would be so wonderful to sing publicly again, wonderful indeed! Vangie had Mama's fragile beauty and nimbleness of fingers with embroidery hoops and needles, but Chris Beth had Mama's voice.

Farmers, cattlemen, and sheepherders alike continued to scan the sky for signs of rain—each in his own way. Abe Solomon claimed that sight of a seagull wheeling this far inland would be a good omen. His wife snorted, "Nonsense! No single way o' tellin' without consultin' the almanac, an' it says the whole year'll be dryer than a bone." Mrs. Malone quoted, "Red sails at night, sailors' delight." To this Brother Amos nodded an agreement: "Yea, ye brethren can discern the face of the sky. 'When it is evening,' quoting from the Good Book, 'it will be fair weather,' ye say, 'for the sky is red.' "

O'Higgin listened with respect, then with merry eyes dancing, announced, " 'Tis a cloud I look for, I be tellin' ye—a wee cloud, sized fer patchin' a Dutchman's pants!"

Equinox came on Sunday. Surely the shifting of the seasons would bring the usual temperamental weather. But housewives turned their calendars from summer to fall and skies remained cloudless.

Joe finished his sermon a little early. It was hot and it was easy to see that the children were restless. Chris Beth found herself wishing again that there were some way to build a church house. Then there could be Sunday school classes for the young people. She secretly had the site chosen. The building just had to nestle among the redbud trees above the ledge and—

Her thinking was cut short by the sudden silence in the group. She realized that Brother Amos was standing, face uplifted and hands raised heavenward. "Hast thou observed what the dust and lack of pure water means? We must prepare for the third plague—sickness and death!"

•   •   •

Dire predictions the settlers did not need. Sickness, Brother Amos had said—and *death*! Some of them believed in "signs." Others did not. "Folklore," they shrugged. But nobody dared dispute the prophesies of the Willow Grove "disciple." Just how he knew was a mystery, but he knew all right. Chris Beth, watching a late September sky—which should have been beautiful but wasn't—wished fervently that she doubted Brother Amos' prophecy of disease. Last September, she remembered, had been glorious. The lowering sun had sent shafts of light through thinning colored boughs of oak and dogwood, which, seen through the thick-needled fir trees, reminded her of stained-glass windows in a great cathedral.

Idly she picked up an eighth-grade reader. She must get at some lesson plans. The addition to the school was progressing nicely and, if she didn't work up a bit of energy, she would be the only person unprepared for opening day.

Something poetic would be nice for the bulletin board—something autumnish. "October is a month of flame—" Oh, dear! She closed the textbook. The only flame was the relentless sun. And it had done more than golden-glow the leaves. The entire countryside was scorched to an ugly brown from its fiery rays. No moisture remained in the air.

Maybe it would be cooler out-of-doors. But no sooner had she settled little Mart on a quilt in the backyard than Vangie's familiar "Yoo-hoo!" signaled a need for her presence at the Big House. Interrupting the baby's game with his fat toes, she scooped him up and hurried across the foot-log.

Vangie's greeting was in breathless, incoherent phrases, characteristic of her speech when she was disturbed. "Scarlet fever's all over the settlement. Doc can't help—has it. And Wilson's packing medicine—what little cure there is. Everything's there—for taking care of True, I mean." She pointed to the bureau and then to the cedar chest. "My uniform—where is it? We may be gone over night. Longer maybe—some have died already and—"

Chris Beth felt herself staring at her sister in horror. 'What can you do? I mean should you go?"

"I should. What's more, I *must*. I'm a nurse. You would,

too—teach, I mean. Why, you'd go into the reservation if they called you. Is my uniform buttoned in back? Anyway, I belong at Wilson's side in sickness and in health and—"

"Stop it, Vangie! You know what I mean. This is dangerous, life-threatening. It *is* infectious?"

"Of course. We'll wear masks—do the best we can. Wilson will take care of me—you know that. You didn't button it. I feel a draft!"

Chris Beth knew a moment's bitterness. Wilson had no right to ask this of Vangie—or even allow it. Vangie was frail herself and prone to contract any disease with which she came in contact. But, yes, she *would* do the same thing—with her teaching or with Joe's ministry.

"Chrissy!" Vangie, looking far too young to wear the professional white uniform, turned to face her. Although her cheeks flushed with excitement, her eyes looked troubled.

"What is it, Vangie? Are you all right?"

"You would take care of True, wouldn't you? If anything—nothing's going to—but if anything *did* happen? You'd tell her—you know—what you feel is best and—promise me?"

"Don't talk like that!" Chris Beth felt the words torn from her lips. Even as she spoke, the men's voices cut through the stale and sultry afternoon air.

"Everything's ready except my Florence Nightingale!" Wilson called from the front yard.

"Promise!" Vangie whispered.

"Oh, Vangie, I promise," Chris Beth whispered in reply and choked back the tears as the four of them embraced. The epidemic had come just as Brother Amos had said.

Young Wil came onto the porch to wave. Thoughtfully he pulled a dried bud which had never had a chance to bloom from the scarlet runner vine. "Will folks die?"

Chris Beth would have tried to shift the conversation, but Joe spoke man-to-man. "I expect so," he said quietly.

"Things would never be the same, would they?"

Young Wil turned tortured eyes to Chris Beth. She longed to comfort this half-man/half-child—to tell him the bad dream would pass. Instead, she answered gently, "No, they never would."

36

Death's Angel

In the days that followed, every home in the settlement was touched by the epidemic. Death's angel seemed to hover overhead, as if undecided which family to visit next. The first one taken was Doc Dullus himself.

When Elmer Goldsmith, who was "runner" for the neighborhood, brought the sad news, Chris Beth's first thought was for Wilson. The old doctor had been like a father.

"Can Wilson manage without him?" She asked Joe through her tears.

"Wilson isn't without him, Chrissy," Joe assured her. "Old Doc left a far greater legacy than instruments and medical books."

That was true, she knew. Wilson had little more than driven away when Joe pointed out the careful list of precautions he had left: "Boil water, bring cow's milk to scalding for babies, soft diet for all (poached eggs, milk toast, custard, rice, broth)...light garments (to be boiled after wear or burned in case of contact with infected patient...)." The list went on and on.

"We'll have to go break the news to O'Higgin and Mrs. Malone," Chris Beth told Joe.

He nodded. Young Wil would look after the babies.

As they approached Turn-Around Inn, the sound of O'Higgin's mellow voice floated across the dry meadows. With a little catch in her throat, Chris Beth remembered Mrs. Malone's words when the Muslin City folk were tuning their fiddles at twilight.

The singing stopped in midmeasure when horse and

riders drew near. O'Higgin's usually merry eyes were grave as he summoned his wife.

"It's Doc—" Joe began.

Mrs. Malones's face blanched, but she raised a hand to stop Joe's words. "Coffee's brewin'," she said briskly, turning toward the door.

Then, over coffee and aged pound cake, the four of them recalled the memories of the lovable doctor—white-whiskered, short and plump, baggy pants tucked into knee-high boots, his cultured voice with its broken English—but, most of all, his medical skill and loving service.

"Best we be preparin' a place. Ye ladies be stayin' here." O'Higgin said.

Joe nodded. "I've put in a lot of time reading up on scarlet fever. The medical journals say to isolate the sick from the well. We *have* to stay on our feet. It's up to us to keep panic down."

"Chrissy—" Joe opened his arms and held her for one sweet moment. O'Higgin attempted a wink, but tears got in the way. Wordlessly he climbed onto Dobbin's back behind Joe.

Quietly the two men buried their beloved friend in a little glade near his house. "Someday," Joe told Chris Beth later, "we'll put up a granite marker. For now there's just a little wooden cross."

Young Elmer's next message was directly from Vangie and Wilson.

"They cain't come home—" the gawkish lad panted, "Cause uv this awful sickness. It took ten more—they was Willis Long, his wife and kids, Otis Flannary—they bein' new—and, oh, yeah, the China-baby—"

"Wong's little sister!" Chris Beth felt as if her heart were in a vise squeezed tighter and tighter. "But—but—"

"Easy, Chrissy, easy," Joe, who was bracing her from behind, whispered against her hair. "Be brave for Elmer and young Wil's sakes."

Chris Beth didn't want to be brave. She wanted to be a little girl cradled in her father's arms, a helpless Southern lady swooning at her husband's feet. She wanted to cry and cry...

Instead, she lifted her shoulders and looked steadily at

the obviously distraught Elmer. "You are a great help, Elmer. Now, can you tell us about the doctor and Miss Vangie?"

"Yessum. That's why I come. They wantin' you should let young Wil come home with me. Then they wantin' you should take the little babies to Miss Mollie—'n you should meet with 'em to help."

Involuntarily Chris Beth's hands went to her face. What if something should happen to the four of them? What would happen to True and little Mart *then*? Surely this was the greatest crisis yet.

In her state of shock and fear, it was not until later she realized that Elmer had said, "They're makin' headquarters at the gen'ral store!"

• • •

Chris Beth closed the door softly behind her, careful not to disturb her sister, and walked to the window of the upstairs room to look out on the dusty street below. Fascinated, she watched a little whirlwind form, dip down, and then drift away. In the same way, she thought sadly, the earthly lives of their family of friends were slipping away. It seemed only natural that she and Vangie should be here together. She, being older, had taken care of Vangie in times of health, so why not in the sickness and death that they were fighting together in the settlement?

Downstairs, Joe would be conferring with Wilson as to how the two of them could be of most help in trying to mend bodies or spirits. Maybe it would be both, she thought, remembering the haggard look of her brother-in-law's face as they entered the general store. And, in her sleep, Vangie—she thought tenderly—looked like a beautiful doll that some thoughtless child had tossed carelessly aside.

She checked her sister's forehead and was relieved to find that it was not feverish.

"You four are welcome to come 'n go as you can. Hope you don't mind sharin' Maggie's room?" Mrs. Solomon had offered.

Chris Beth was sure her surprise showed, for the woman continued, "She won't be comin' 'round. Run off with a

stocking drummer—after all her pa and me's done for th'
girl."

"I'm sorry."

Mrs. Solomon turned away, but not before Chris Beth saw
the tears. "She'd made her bed. Let her lie in it!" she said
brusquely.

When Vangie awakened, her first question was about
True. Chris Beth assured her that all was well at home. Then
the two of them talked about the epidemic. "It's bad—oh,
it's bad," Vangie's lip quivered, but her chin was raised
in determination. "The Smiths lost one of the twins and
the other is very low. Oh, Chrissy, are you *sure* True's all
right?"

"Right as rain," she smiled, "But are *you*?"

Vangie pushed back a curl and nodded. "But we need
help. Wilson may not let you go inside, but if you can count
out pills, take care of children, call on the ones who've had
deaths in the family—"

"All of those. We're survivors, you and I. Haven't we
proved that already?"

Vangie let two fat tears roll down her cheeks then, the
way she always did as a little girl. "You always make me
feel better. And we will survive. We have to. With God's
help."

"With God's help," Chris Beth repeated, "We will lick
this epidemic."

37

Why, Lord? Why?

Time lost all meaning. How long had they been battling the epidemic, anyway? Two weeks? Or was it months? Or years? Chris Beth hardly noticed whether it was day or night. At Joe's urging, she ate. Under Wilson's watchful eye, she scrubbed herself raw. And she must have talked. People, whose faces she scarcely saw through her fatigue, kept telling her what a comfort she was. But what had she said? Even the pain and the fear she had felt when the scarlet fever first broke out was softened by a merciful kind of numbness around her heart.

Her only emotion was a gnawing sense of emptiness at being unable to see little Mart. "Couldn't you do without me just a few hours?" she begged.

"Actually, no" Wilson answered the question she had directed to Joe. "But that's not the point. We can't risk spreading this thing. So far we're holding our own."

"Maybe Mrs. Malone could at least get some word to me."

"Absolutely not!" And then his tone softened. "I'm sorry. I understand, you know."

Of course, he did. But the ache would not go away.

"Are we winning?" she asked Wilson on another occasion.

"It's hard to tell. I'm beginning to think scarlet fever's not a disease but more a form of streptococci—sometimes it's the fever and sometimes in the same family it's a mild sore throat. Material for my next book—if we can just hang on here—"

The pink light of dawn crept in to touch Maggie's bed, where Chris Beth and Vangie had stretched out just two

160

hours before. A shower of pebbles shattered the stillness. Still enveloped in a fog of sleep, Chris Beth dragged herself to the window. Joe stood motioning below. His waving was unnecessary. The toss of pebbles could only mean, "Another case. Another emergency. Come!"

Even as she turned to waken Vangie, Chris Beth saw the ancient carriage, its windows draped in black crepe. Its passing meant that Wilson had lost another patient. Another family circle broken. And nobody to mourn the passing except the grieving loved ones. Others looked out, white-faced, through their windows, wondering, "Why, Lord, why?"

● ● ●

"Whose house?" Chris Beth asked woodenly.

"Two families occupy it," Joe explained as he helped her and Vangie from the buggy. "Boones, relatives of Orin and Susanah R-Robbins."

Joe stumbled over the name. Probably he had wanted to spare her any embarrassment. But didn't he know that she was feeling nothing these days? Nothing, that is, except for the driving urge to do what she could for the living. Go home. See the baby. Get on with life.

Wilson, having given up trying to protect even herself and Vangie, let alone himself and Joe, hurried inside the cabin. Wordlessly the rest of them followed. At the door, Joe stopped to tack up the dreaded sign: QUARANTINE, DO NOT ENTER! lettered in red. Numbly Chris Beth adjusted her mask and murmured a little disjointed prayer: "Please, Lord, spare as many as You can— please, Lord." Then, squaring her shoulders, she moved through the door, wondering how soon the quarantine sign would be replaced with black crepe and which of the two families would be taken away in the funeral carriage.

After a quick, professional check of the others, Wilson moved to where Susanah lay motionless and still. A telltale frown crossed his brow. "Susanah?" When there was no answer, Wilson began his quiet instructions, his tone diagnosing to the three who worked with him, "Scarlet fever." And his eyes communicated, "No hope."

All day the four of them worked with Susanah. "You'll have to help us," Wilson kept repeating to his weakening patient, but there was no response. She seemed not to move at all except for labored breathing.

Chris Beth left the bedside, where Vangie wiped the woman's fevered brow. Cold with apprehension, she tried to speak calmly to the children who kept trying to crowd into the small room. Death was inevitable for Susanah, and Chris Beth did not want the young ones on hand.

"Come and let me show you a finger game," Chris Beth told the children "If you are very quiet, you can play it by yourselves."

When she was sure they were diverted, Chris Beth tip-toed silently back to where Wilson, Vangie, and Joe were leaning over the sickbed.

"Don't try to talk," Wilson said gently. "Go to sleep."

Susanah's face was wax-white and there was a faint blue tint to her lips, through which she was trying to whisper a message. Then, feebly, she motioned to Vangie.

"Forgive me—I didn't know—" She fought laboriously for breath. "I meant no harm—forgive me—her, too—"

Vangie dropped to her knees and, with tears streaming down her face, cradled the dying woman's head gently in her arms. "It's all right," she soothed, "oh, my darling, it's all right."

Vangie shouldn't be so close to Susanah—and her mask has slipped down, Chris Beth thought numbly. Foolishly, as if it would help, she reached out in an effort to adjust the shield. Inside, she knew that it was more than the disease from which she wished to protect Vangie and herself. Vangie looked helpless and frightened, but she shrugged off her sister's hand. Then a small sigh said Susanah was gone.

"Susanah!" The word was torn from Vangie's lips. And then she turned to Chris Beth for comfort. Both of them gave way to their grief as the men covered Susanah's now-peaceful face and spoke quiet words of consolation to Orin.

38

Hiyiu Cultus Seek!

In the hot, orange twilight, Wilson and Vangie hurried away on another call. Chris Beth remained behind with Joe to try to bring comfort to the home that death had touched.

Olivia Boone, looking little and frightened, asked haltingly, "What can I do?" And then she burst into tears. "I wish I were home. We never should have come. I'll catch the next wagon train—"

"Get a grip on yourself!" Chris Beth used her schoolteaching voice in order to stem the other woman's hysteria. "You'll adjust here. We'll help you. And there's no way a wagon train will be allowed to pass until the quarantine's lifted. The streets are deserted." Then, adding more gently, she said, "Let's sit down."

With calm deliberation, she smoothed Olivia's brown hair from her pale face. And, working to control her own anxieties, Chris Beth tried to think and speak as Mrs. Malone would have—soothingly, calmly.

Did she know where Susanah's Sunday dress was hanging? The two of them must wash her face and fluff her hair. The men would prepare the grave...too far to take the body to Graveyard Creek Cemetery. Too dark. Too dangerous.

Couldn't they wait until tomorrow? Shouldn't there be a wake?

No, the burial must take place immediately. And no callers could come. The house was quarantined.

Move...move...don't think...just pray! Finally something resembling order came to the house, and then a kind of peace. Chris Beth realized with a strange kind of exhilaration that an onlooker would never suspect that she had not dealt directly with death before.

Chris Beth helped to put the children in bed before burial of the body took place. She and Olivia held lanterns for the men to see by. It was with a great sense of relief that she saw a flush of dawn in the eastern sky. Surely today would be better. *Anyway*, she thought, *the Lord has shown me that I can do what I have to do!*

But soon enough she was to wonder about that. First there was the muted sound of running footsteps and then an eerie scream. Out of nowhere came the swift-moving shadow of a near-nude figure. An Indian! But before the astonished group could grasp the situation, the man was speaking, "*Hiyiu cultus seek!* Come!"

Boston Buck! Remembering her one encounter with the young brave, Chris Beth felt fear vibrate up and down her spine. The sweating russet-brown body advanced. The intense, dark eyes sought hers desperately. "Come. *Seek!*" And he pointed to the forest in the general direction of the reservation.

Olivia's husband and Orin Robbins lifted their shovels. But Joe put up a restraining hand. "There's unrest already. Be careful!" Then, to Boston Buck, he said, "Sickness? Yes, I will go with you."

The young Indian crossed his arms and waited before speaking. Then, "Bring *Black Book* and squaw!" he said.

Joe must have sensed her apprehension. "Evil spirits," he told her in a low tone when Boston Buck suddenly increased his speed to outdistance the riders.

Soundlessly, Boston Buck ran ahead of the horses. How fleet of foot he was! But why did he choose the more open woods or skirt the woods completely whenever possible and stare uneasily into the dark, thick forest stretches? Once Chris Beth had feared the young brave himself. Now she was more afraid of what *he* feared. Wild animals? Warriors from other tribes?

Then suddenly they were in an Indian village. But how strange! The huts were made of crude shakes cut from fir trees instead of animal skins as geography books had described them. And the buildings were stuck here and there beneath a bluff instead of being a part of the reservation just beyond. This could mean only one thing. Boston Buck must be the son of Chief Halo. Wilson had told her about the old Indian chief. He was shunned by other tribes because of his near-white skin and was called Halo (meaning poor) because he had few dogs or ponies, only one squaw, and only one son.

Chris Beth's fragmented thinking was interrupted by the sudden stop of the horses. Boston Buck blocked the way as he pointed with ill-concealed pride to his village. "*Splachta alla*," he said.

"Home in a sheltered vale," Joe interpreted with a nod.

The young Indian then pointed to the reservation. "*Nika wake clatawa!*"

Joe hesitated, then asked haltingly, "I—will—not—go?"

This time it was the Indian who nodded. Then he *was* Halo's son!

Chris Beth's mind resumed its jumbled thinking. Better here than on the reservation—maybe. But if only Wilson were here—he understands. And, anyway, a doctor is needed. What can *we* do? Any action may endanger our lives. After all, Boston Buck's the chief now...and a chief's a chief—even if He's the son of a poor one! The fever will spread and—

There was no time to think further. Already Joe was helping her to the ground. Then, with Boston Buck in the lead, they entered the largest of the huts just as the sun touched its dry-moss roof.

Several women squatted around the central fire, stirring something that smelled of fish. It was hard to breathe. Chris Beth's lungs were filled with smoke. And surely she was going to be sick from the smell and drying skins. Fatigue gripped her body. Fear clutched her heart. The room and all its horrors reeled crazily.

"Steady," Joe whispered. "If it's too much—"

His words were interrupted by a low moan from a crude bench along a wall opposite the room's only door. Reflex action took her forward. When Joe would have followed, Boston Buck restrained him.

"Squaw stay! You come!"

Chris Beth did not know what she had expected. A small child, most likely. Critically ill of scarlet fever. Instead, the writhing body of a young Indian woman lay on the animal skin. And she was trying to give birth to a child! Automatically she waved Joe out with Boston Buck. At least she wouldn't have to contend with a witchdoctor. And the other women had been unable to deliver the baby. Small comfort! What could *she* do? But they trusted her.

"You'll have to help me this time, Lord!" she prayed aloud desperately. To the other women, she said, *"Pray!"* Their only response was to cringe back in fear. She tried again, reaching arms heavenward. "Great—White—Spirit," she said slowly. And, at that signal, the women began a strange chant, otherworldly in Chris Beth's ears but apparently soothing to her patient, who seemed to relax slightly.

"Hot water," she whispered to one of the younger girls, spreading her hands over the fire to communicate.

The girl understood. Hurriedly she brought a tightly woven basked filled with water and set it beside the fire. Then, with two sticks, she lifted hot rocks and dropped them one by one into the basket. There was a hiss of steam and then the water began to boil.

Hour after hour the two of them worked over the laboring woman. Time and time again, Chris Beth thought they were losing the battle. Then something of what Wilson had taught her when they brought little True into the world came back.

"Push...relax...push..." she instructed, demonstrating her meaning. "And you—" Turning to her helper, she hesitated, wishing she knew her name.

To her surprise, the girl answered "White Arms" in a small voice.

"You, White Arms, bathe her face like this. Then hold *her*—"

"Boston Girl."

"Hold Boston Girl when I say—like this. Push...relax... push...*Hold her*—Oh, *Lord, help us!*...Push...relax...push..."

Through the white maze into which her mind had blessedly taken refuge, Chris Beth heard the unceasing chant of the women's prayer, the occasional bark of a dog, the raucous call of a jay, and Joe's voice. He seemed to be reading—but what? She only knew that each time his voice, now hoarse, stopped, Boston Buck commanded, "Read more. Heap more. Boston Buck want *Talking Book*."

Talking Book? The Bible! "The Lord is my Shepherd..." On and on Joe read. Then, as the evening sun dipped into the Western sky, Chris Beth emerged from behind the skin covering the door of the hut. "Come in and meet the new chief!" she invited a beaming Boston Buck calmly. Then, weeping, she collapsed into Joe's arms.

$$\bullet \quad \bullet \quad \bullet$$

At the edge of the woods, the exhausted pair spotted a lone rider. Chris Beth scarcely recognized the strained, white face in the gathering twilight. But it was—it had to be—Wilson! Fear clutched her heart. Where was Vangie? What was he doing out here without the buggy?

"Vangie? Where's Vangie?" She cried out even as dust choked back her words.

Wilson reined in beside her and Joe. "What are *you* doing here?" His voice sounded angry. "Do you realize how dangerous this could have been, Joe? And you, you blessed idiot—" He looked at Chris Beth.

If I didn't know him better, I'd think he was going to cry, her tired mind thought. But what about Vangie.

"Vangie? *Wilson!*"

But Wilson turned to Joe. "Don't you realize—"he started to ask again.

"How dangerous it was, " Joe finished. "Yes, but don't *you* realize how dangerous it would have been *not* to come? We have to minister to them all. The Lord didn't specify which color."

"I didn't mean that and you know it. I mean the hostility—and now the spread of this epidemic."

"No epidemic," Joe said. "A baby."

"*Vangie!*" Chris Beth's patience had snapped.

"A baby yet. You delivered a *baby*? How convenient."

Without warning, Chris Beth's anger turned to quiet desperation. She simply dropped her head and let tears of exhaustion roll down her face unchecked. It didn't matter. Something had happened to Vangie.

For the first time, neither of the men seemed to notice. they were engaged in a subject and she had missed part of it.

"You mean she's *there*? Is she going to be all right?"

"She wants to see Chris Beth."

Then, as if seeing her for the first time, both of them turned to Chris Beth. "Vangie fainted and I took her in—"

"*Fainted*? Oh, Wilson, does she have the bad kind—I mean—"

"No, the *good* kind. I'm so glad you're getting experience at midwifery. Your little sister is going to have a baby!"

• • •

Even before she saw his ebony face, wreathed in welcoming smiles, Chris Beth knew that the cabin the three of them reached just had to be Ole Tobe's, the black man who had brought the donkey to the Christmas program. "Coffee!" Wilson sniffed with appreciation. Joe said, "Spice something or other?" "Molasses cookies," Chris Beth replied. But neither the wild beauty of the place nor the tantalizing odors held as much fascination for her as the mellow crooning coming from the cabin door. "Thet's the Sleepy Hollow tune, lika colohed mammy's croon to her sleepy lit-tle pick-an-ny on uh lazy aftahnoon..."

The voice! The slurring of the vowels and softening of the consonants, even the song itself! It had to be—it *had* to be—"Aunt Mandy." The wonderful mammy who had been more a mother to her than Mama!

Brushing past Ole Tobe, Chris Beth rushed into the room, where the ample-bosomed woman, her face partially hidden, leaned over Vangie's sleeping figure on the small cot. But her trained ear picked up the footsteps and, pushing a wisp of now-graying hair beneath the red bandanna, she turned the familiar, lovable face toward any intruder who dared wake her "baby."

A finger warned for silence. Then slowly it went down when the woman saw Chris Beth. The wonderful woman from a childhood past rushed forward. "Oh, praise de Lawd! He dun sent my Miss Chrissy back."

With a cry of delight, Chris Beth raced into the out-stretched arms. "Oh, Aunt Mandy, Aunt Mandy—how? Oh, Aunt Mandy—"

"Don' you cry now, honey chile. Ain't ever gonna be no more tears fer you 'n me. Shh-h-h, y'all don wanna be wakin' yah baby sistah!"

Vangie slept through the reunion. Chris Beth was glad. So much needed asking and explaining. Why hadn't Aunt Mandy come to last year's Christmas program when Ole Tobe brought the sheep? *Us colohed folks ain't always welcome, chile.* Oh, things are different here—no need coming in back doors either! But how did this miracle happen?

Atlanta ain't de same since de burnin', dun drove us outta our homes. Me'n my man up 'n jumped de broom and comed West. Praise de Lawd!

39

Fire

The epidemic ended as abruptly as it began. Loss of life was "considerably light," city doctors told Wilson. The letter of congratulations was waiting at the general store when he, Chris Beth, and Joe returned to Centerville. What's more, the letter went on, if he wished to pursue his findings on "isolating the sick from the well," and continue his dissertation on "Streptococci, Species of," they could, under "certain circumstances," arrange a loan for him.

When Chris Beth and Joe would have interrupted with whoops of joy, Wilson put up his hand with a grin. "There's more! I received an advance royalty check on the botany book. And this is for you."

Joe accepted the envelope, then handed it to Chris Beth. Puzzled by the crude printing, she ripped the letter open. Inside was a vague note from Nate Goldsmith saying that the State of Oregon was helping out with schools, and would this be acceptable by her? *Acceptable?* A $100- warranty marked "For Services to Be Rendered"!

As if that weren't enough, Abe Solomon (being "duly appointed by the actin' board o' deacons," he explained) handed a mysterious-looking little packet to Joe the day following.

"Money!" Joe gasped when several large bills spilled out.

"Cash money, no less!" Abe said proudly. "From us all. And don't go sayin' you cain't accept it and you're doin' the Lord's work. It's from our tithes and offerings. Then John Henry Dobbs sold his hawgs."

"How will I ever get it all written in my diary?" Vangie laughed when they went to pick her up two days later.

170

There was more. But now was not the time to share it, Chris Beth decided. While Joe and Wilson made final calls (and she was supposed to be resting?), she had slipped out the side door of the store and paid a visit to the office marked ASSAYER. Just how much, she wondered, would a pearl-and-sapphire brooch which she described be worth? The little man, wearing a dark sunshade and clamping a mouthful of gold teeth on a cigar which had long since gone out, looked at her cagily. Not much, most likely, he parried. As she was about to leave, he said, not to get too hasty. Could do a *little* better—if she would like to bring it in. Matter of fact, he hoped she *would* bring it. "And real soon, eh, lovely lady?"

Aunt Mandy wept when her "babies" left but smiled broadly when Vangie told her that she would be calling on her for help when the second baby came. Ole Tobe said he'd help buildin' on the school.

The buggy was packed. Dobbin was saddled. Good-byes were finished. Or so Chris Beth thought. She had forgotten Mrs. Solomon—or maybe she had supposed that thanking the woman who had been so kind was enough.

"Don't go bein' so hurried!" Bertie's voice was gruff in an effort to hide her tears. "Here's our tithes. Abe and me, we figured you'd be needin' some staples. They're sorta to thank you fer—fer bein' here and takin' the sting out o' Maggie's leavin'. Now take 'em and git!"

● ● ●

"Wolf" spotted the group and alerted the Mahoney-O'Higgin tribe. The geese sounded their alarm. And children descended upon Chris Beth, Vangie, Joe, and Wilson from all directions, all talking at once.

"School's beautiful...some of the men's gone workin' on the railroad...what'll we do 'bout a church if Miss Mollie and O'Higgin make Turn-Around Inn into a *real* inn? Yes, the stage is comin', too—Miss Mollie read me 'bout it in the Portland newspaper...Andy's got a pet crow... O'Higgin says it can talk if we'll let him split its tongue, but Miss Mollie says the only one in need of splittin's *his*!

"Shoo! Ever' one of you, *shoo* this minute. I declare they'll talk a leg off'n a body."

But Mrs. Malone had handed an unbelievably bigger Mart, his face rosy with a recent nap, to Chris Beth. As she pressed her face against little Mart's fuzzy head, it wouldn't have mattered one bit how much the children talked or what they said. "My baby! My baby! Oh, thank You, Lord," she whispered over and over.

Through a maze of happiness, she managed a meal (never remembering what she ate), greeted young Wil when he and Elmer appeared on schedule, exchanged greetings with O'Higgin, and said good-byes. And then, blessedly, they were home.

• • •

An early frost turned the few remaining leaves scarlet and the wild apples along the fence rows to pure gold. There had been no rain to wash down the suspended smoke and dust particles. So the valley was wrapped in a gossamer shawl of Indian summer. The hollows echoed with the hammering of the woodpeckers and the chattering of the gray squirrels as they graveled the forest paths with the hulls of acorns and hazelnuts.

Out of the autumn haze, Elmer Goldsmith raced all over the settlement on the last Saturday in October. "Think you can squeeze into shoes next Monday?" Chris Beth teased the panting boy.

Elmer blushed. "I'll try, Miss Chrissy—and you'n ever'body else's supposed t' come to Turn-Around Inn tomorrow—church 'n all, then dinner. More'n that, though, it's a Thanksgivin', you know, 'bout the sickness goin' away—and I'll be there, too."

"Not unless you slow down. Have some grape juice before you go."

The crowd gathered early. The Craigs and the Norths were there ahead of the others. There was so much talking to do. As it turned out, most of the words were left unsaid.

Mrs. Malone and O'Higgin were engaged in a heated discussion about the season—too pleasant, by far, to be interrupted.

"*Second summer*, I declare it to be, " Mrs. Malone said.

"Sure'n a *squaw summer* to the likes o' ye!" O'Higgin's deep voice boomed back.

By then the crowd filled the house, with each person bringing another story as to how Indian summer came to be.

"Smoke came from Indian signals and hung in the heavens, proclaiming the last war, so I hear," Joe said with a smile.

"Not so," Wilson denied with a sober face. Then, imitating O'Higgin's Irish brogue as best he could, he added, "Be ye not knowin' now it came from Ireland, it did? Spread from the Emerald Isle to Canada—"

The others laughed. But something in the air bothered Chris Beth. Could be, she thought it was only the talk that made her imagine she smelled smoke. At first it was like the scent of drying apples. Then her nostrils picked up what reminded her of the sweet-smoke smell that came from the controlled burning-off of the cured sugar cane just before it was cut for the mill...the time when Mama didn't worry if she cut through the woods. Hornets were at peace and chances were good that the snakes had crawled away to hibernate...

Her thinking was cut short. *Smoke!* She smelled real smoke.

Fire. The house was on fire! "Fire!" Chris Beth screamed the single-word warning and was sorry immediately. The result was mayhem. Panic-stricken, the worshipers rushed outside. Guided by emotion instead of reason, their instinct was to get home to protect their own homes. *They're leaving us* was all she could think. *In a burning house—*

The rest was like a horrible nightmare. "Giddyup!" Helplessly she watched one wagon after another rush away. Teams, urged by overexcited drivers and the scent of smoke, snorted, pitched, and strained in the harness. Chris could only stand and stare in horrible fascination as one wagon went out of control, spilling its occupants to the ground, and then collided with another wagon.

Then her voice came. "Help!" she screamed. Why wasn't Joe at her side? Wilson—Vangie, where was Vangie? *The babies!* "Help!" she screamed again before rushing up the stairs to the upper room.

As she took the steps two at a time, somehow Chris Beth's reeling senses began to right themselves. Her first real focus of awareness was the odd yellowish glow of sun which, through the haze of smoke, tried to light the upstairs room of the inn. Then she saw Vangie.

"True and little Mart are all right," Vangie's voice spoke through the eerie light.

"Oh, thank God!" Chris Beth grabbed little Mart from Vangie's arms and the two of them descended the stairs hurriedly with the sleeping babies. Only then did Chris Beth realize that the fire was not inside the building. "Where then—"

She must have spoken, for Vangie was sobbing, "It—it's everywhere! The whole world's on fire! *Wilson!*"

"He's helpin' the needy ones close at hand," Mrs. Malone spoke from the bottom of the stairs. "Worst of the fire's to th' east. Problem bein' we've got an easterly wind risin'— you children come back here this minute!"

To the east, billows of black smoke belched from the mountains, Chris Beth saw from the front window. More frightening was the line of fire spreading through the trees, its hungry tongues licking at the dry forest floor and— unsatisfied—lapping at the lifeless meadows below. In the split second that Chris Beth watched numbly, the winds lifted sparks from the site and sent them spinning into adjoining groves. There was a booming explosion on contact and a firestorm roared through the treetops. And cabins! Cabins were burning...*lives were in danger...*

A new spiral of smoke caught her eye—closer. There was something they should be doing. She realized then that Mrs. Malone and Vangie had gone into the kitchen. She must follow. But as she turned, Chris Beth realized that she had seen a lone figure—or thought she had—standing motionless at the edge of the clearing. She looked to be sure, and what she saw brought her senses back completely.

"Joe!" She may have screamed the word, because suddenly Vangie and Mrs. Malone were at her side. "Joe!" Chris Beth heard her voice rise. "Something's wrong with Joe!"

"Joe's all right—" Mrs. Malone tried to soothe. "He's there—"

"He's *not* all right! Or he wouldn't just stand there! Take the baby—no don't! I want him with me—"

Aware that two pairs of arms were trying to restrain her, Chris Beth jerked free. "Try to be calm," Mrs. Malone begged. "Let me—"

"I can't be calm any longer! Flood—plague—epidemic—and now *this*!" Yes, *this* was the worst of all. She knew instinctively what was wrong with Joe. He was in a state of shock at the sight of fire—remembering, beyond all doubt, the inferno which had taken his childhood home, his mother, his father—and had shaken his faith in God and left him an emotional cripple at the very mention of the word.

"Chrissy, no!" But Chris Beth ignored her sister's warning cries and raced toward Joe, covering little Mart's face with her sunbonnet to protect him from the smoke as she ran.

Heat like the blast of a furnace rushed ahead of the main blaze. Above the roar of the fire, deafening explosions told of more and more firestorms. And then there was the unmistakable wail of a baby!

"Joe, Joe!" she tried to scream above the force of the rising wind. But her voice was sucked away. With a sob she reached out to Joe to shake him, to arouse him, to alert him to danger. She tugged at his arm, crying out words she never remembered...how much she loved him...needed him...how much God needed him to save the baby...

"The *baby*!" Joe still stood as if paralyzed, but he had heard. Oh, praise the Lord, he had *heard*!

"A baby, Joe" she sobbed, "a baby! A baby's in the cabin—burning—a *baby*—"

"I have to go. I *h-have* t-to g-go." Joe spoke the words as though he scarcely believed them. But he was breathing. He was alive again. "I have to go, Darling." Suddenly, as if alerted to danger for the first time, Joe spoke to her. "Go back to safety. I have to go."

Then, with his face protected only by his arms, Joe raced through the smoke toward the cabin less than a hundred yards away.

Chris Beth realized suddenly what she had done. She had sent Joe into a burning building. She had asked him—*forced* him—to risk his life. If anything happened, it would be her fault. "Oh, dear God," she whispered, "what have I done?"

Smoke swirled around her, choking her, causing little Mart to fret. She swayed dizzily on her feet. "Don't cry, Darling. We'll go back soon, but we can't leave Daddy now." She stood rooted, unable to move as, through the thickening smoke, she saw Joe try the front door of the cabin. When it didn't yield, he kicked it open.

"Joe—Joe—*don't*!"

But, like a swimmer preparing for a deep dive, Joe appeared to take a deep breath and then plunged inside. No more than seconds passed, Chris Beth knew later, but it seemed a lifetime before his familiar face, blackened almost beyond recognition, loomed out of the smoke. *He didn't even have his face covered*, she thought numbly.

Then something inside her snapped. "Joe!" she screamed his name again and again as she saw him stagger from the cabin and then collapse. She must help him. She must take the little blanket-covered figure from his arms. Chris Beth raced toward his crumpled form. "Please, Lord, please let me be in time." But what held her back?

"Get back! Get back, you little idiot!" The voice was Wilson's. And the arms that held her were his. And she was being soundly shaken by capable hands that knew how to hold a baby and his mother together. "Snap out of it! This is not time for hysteria. Get to the inn so I can help Joe. Gather blankets—food—water—if we can save the place, it'll have to serve as emergency headquarters. Are you all right?"

She nodded. Yes, she was all right. And Joe would be, too. All right in every way. In control, she turned toward the inn and ran. Looking back, she saw O'Higgin join Wilson. The two of them disappeared in Joe's direction as the scene was swallowed in a wall of flame.

Vangie and Mrs. Malone met her halfway and the three of them ran across the fields to the temporary safety of Turn-Around Inn.

"Sniff this!" Mrs. Malone ordered, forcing an ammonia-soaked cloth beneath Chris Beth's nose. "Th' Lord'll protect our menfolk."

Her head, if not her heart, cleared. Move...don't think...move...and *pray*! And, through it all, the wild feeling, "I've been through it before—too many times." Move...don't think...move...*pray*!

"Get the coffeepot boilin', girls. One of you slice the bread and spread it with butter—thick-like. Vangie, what medications do we need from the chest?"

Vangie stopped crying and was suddenly the nurse. "Bandages—you can roll them, Chrissy. Blankets for shock—*all* the blankets, quilts—even sheets—soap, hot water, turpentine—"

The three of them made every preparation they could. Maybe, just maybe it would work, providing the house stood. Mustn't think about that. Just draw water from the well. Fill every tub and basin. Wet down the roof as far as they could reach. Spread wet sacks over the doors and windows...and move...don't think...*pray*!

"I've had quite a talk with You, Lord," Chris Beth heard herself whisper over and over. "Save us. Bring the men back. Give me strength."

Wordlessly they worked on until, above the roar of the fast-approaching fire, there was a deafening explosion. It couldn't be. But it was! Thunder—and before there was time to absorb the suddenness of an approaching storm, there was a blinding flash of lightning that might well have heralded the end of the world. And then the rains came! In blinding sheets. By the bucket. By the barrel! And Vangie, so terrified of storms, didn't even whimper!

The three women danced wildly in a circle in the front room, stopping only long enough to embrace one another. "We prayed for this," Mrs. Malone said. "And the Lord answered in His own good time!"

40

Up from the Ashes

A gentle, familiar squeeze of her hand awakened Chris Beth. Joe's face swam into focus. A shaft of sun touched his tousled hair with bronze. Did her husband or did he not wear a halo? Well, he deserved one—but what on earth were they doing on their knees? *Ouch!* She tried to pull herself up.

"Easy," he whispered. Only then did she realize that the two of them held hands over several sleeping children. "We've been here a long time."

She nodded and both of them smiled, remembering. "Right back where we started," she said. "It was here that you proposed during the flood—but, oh, Joe—the babies—our cabin—?"

"Safe. All safe. Saved by the rain and the grace of God! The fire tooks its toll—houses, livestock, timber—but no lives, and we have a lot of persons deserving praise. Including our junior deacon!"

How well she knew! Why, young Wil had been a modern-day Paul Revere. No amount of reasoning could have stopped the lad from doing his service to the Lord as he understood it. Oh, how she loved him—as much as if he were her very own.

"He's growing remarkably," she said, making an effort to stand.

"Aren't we all?" Joe whispered softly. "You were wonderful last night."

Last night. It all came back in a flash. The fire...her fear, which dissolved into nothingness like a wisp of morning fog, in the face of Joe's greater fear...then his safe return...the look of victory on his face...and the night—so horrible and yet so wonderful—which brought them together closer to each other and to the Lord than they had ever been before.

"Wonderful?" Chris Beth smiled at her husband's compliment. "I guess we all were. I wonder how many people we tried to help. You mean they *all* will make it?"

Joe nodded. "A miracle. And, as to how many, I lost count. But together, Chrissy, we coped."

His eyes sought hers and her heart was too full to answer. It was enough that they understood each other. Yes, together they had coped.

"You two gonna talk all day or would you like t' partake of some vittles?" Mrs. Malone asked quietly from the door.

"Sourdough biscuits 'n honey ye be havin'!" O'Higgin promised. "Sure'n the coffee be a strong brew. Took Doc Wilson 'n Miss Vangie home, it did!"

Chris Beth tried unsuccessfully to smooth her hair, which had managed to come unbraided during the long dark night. Then, cautiously, she and Joe picked their way over sleeping bodies and followed O'Higgin and Mrs. Malone down the stairs.

"Th' good Lord only knows how many lives the four of you saved last night. Could've been a holocaust without Wilson and Vangie's doctorin' and comfortin' from the two o' you." Mrs. Malone poured coffee.

Chris took a bracing gulp. "We had help," she said, meaning it both ways.

Later, looking at the black, ghostlike statues of what only hours before were beautiful green fir trees whose needles whispered a song, Chris Beth thought her heart would break. The trees were the beauty, the pride, the very livelihood of the settlement. But they were more than that to her. It was their song she remembered most—their soothing lullaby, the song that calmed her in time of crisis and whispered of eternity when earthly life tested her faith. Now the forest was silent. Maybe the gnarled, black branches could never sing again. "Oh, no!" she whispered.

"Now, now," Mrs. Malone said from behind her. "Nature

has a way o' restorin' itself. You'll see." Then, shifting the subject, the practical woman said, "It's my drapes nature cain't restore. Just you come 'n look what that Irishman done with my drapes!"

Chris Beth looked, and what she saw hurt her almost as much as the sight of the dead forest. Mrs. Malone's green brocade drapes, her pride and joy, lay crumpled, water-soaked, and blook-stained on the floor of the front room. Obviously, having run out of blankets for wrapping those in shock or with their clothing burned off completely, O'Higgin had jerked down the draperies and put them to use.

"Oh, Mrs. Malone, I'm so sorry—" But Mrs. Malone turned and walked inside. Chris Beth knew the sign. It meant that the matter was closed. But for herself it was not. She and Vangie might have a plan...

• • •

November came with a bright-blue countenance. Little tributaries, fed by the autumn rains and laughing themselves right out of their banks, hurried to join the larger creeks and rivers. Thirst was quenched in the settlement—the old orchards to the south, the meadows to the north, and the tangled dogwood, laurel, manzanita, and firs which the fire had spared to the east and west. Why did so many people persist in calling autumn a season of sadness? Chris Beth wondered as she looked out the cabin window. "Even in its charred condition, the valley is filled with promise," she mused. "Nature's only sleeping...it's the seventh day of creation and God is resting."

"But not so with the rest of us!" Joe's voice startled her.

"I didn't know I spoke aloud."

"I'm glad. It gave your whereabouts away. And I've been wanting to talk with you—privately."

"Joe—" She would have pulled away, but his strong arms imprisoned her from behind. "Let go—there's so much to do. School will be opening in a month—you know that it's only because of the fire that they postponed the opening and—"

Joe laughed at her rushing words. *We know each other*

so well, she thought dreamily. *He's aware that I talk too fast when I know what he's about to say. And I do know!*

"Do I have to act like a caveman? You know, grab you by the hair and drag you into a cave to teach you a lesson? Or do we start a family soon?"

"As soon as I learn how to knit."

"That will be forever," he moaned.

"Not on your life! Mrs. Malone's teaching me. Which reminds me, Joe—seriously, now—I need some yarn. Couldn't we go into Centerville tomorrow?"

"Oh, by all means! And with that promise, I will even release you—temporarily. That is, after a kiss?"

Chris Beth turned to give him a grateful hug. She did want to pick up some yarn. But she wanted to talk with the assayer too....

*   *   *

Joe was right, Chris Beth realized, as the weeks passed. The settlers certainly were not resting. And, for that matter, neither was the Lord! He was greening up the meadows and opening the windows of heaven to let down exactly the right amount of rain—not enough to overflow the rivers, but just enough to furnish all the needs for next year's crops and to give O'Higgin just cause to predict (as he had earlier in the year) that sure to come was the most bountiful harvest ever. Even Brother Amos took to saying, "The lean times are past and fat times lie ahead if thou wilt but put thy trust in the Lord and thy hand to the plow!"

"Well, us folks're doin' both, wouldn't you say, Brother Joseph?" Nate Goldsmith asked at one of the roof-raisings where neighbors gathered to complete a new cabin.

"That I would," Joe agreed. "The school's coming along fine too, thanks to all the lumber donated by newcomers on the ledge. God surely must have intended their belt of timber to be spared."

"With equal thanks to them that hauled th' logs," Nate added significantly. "My team included. Y'knew the storehouse was comin' along, too, what with Brother Amos supervisin' and all—say, best we be plannin' that thanksgivin' meetin' that the fires interrupted, huh? Guess

I'll up 'n call a deacons' meetin' soon. This way we can give praise on the *real* Thanksgivin'!"

● ● ●

Thanksgiving Day dawned cobalt-blue—a day just right, the settlers agreed as they gathered in full force at Turn-Around Inn, for man and "all them over which he has dominion" to give praise to their Creator. Chris Beth had never been happier as she, Joe, Wilson, Vangie, and their combined families piled into the buggy and headed for the place so dear to their hearts: Turn-Around Inn, where miracles happened! And today would be no exception, she thought with a surge of joy. In fact, it well might be the day of the greatest miracle of all. Certainly she hugged the germ of one close to her heart. And she suspected that each member in the Craig-North party possessed one too. Never had she seen such secretiveness except at Christmastime.

The only touch of sadness she felt was the thought of Maggie Solomon. The news "Maggie's back" ran like wildfire all over Centerville. "Yeah, stockin' drummer up 'n dumped 'er. Bitter pill fer Abe 'n Bertie t' swallow, sure enough." Chris Beth had walked away from such talk, but she wondered if the girl would have the courage to show up today.

"Are you all right?" Chris Beth realized guiltily that with all the demands that other people had placed on her she had had little time to devote to her sister. They had hardly had time to discuss her good news.

Vangie laughed. "Never been better. You know pregnancy always becomes me. Doubly so this time. I plan on twins, you know—a dimpled, roly-poly frog-prince like little Mart and a fairy princess like True!"

Turn-Around Inn, looking clean and inviting in its setting of new-green meadows, loomed ahead. Young Wil whistled. "Look at the crowd!" And then they were surrounded by their loving family of friends.

O'Higgin's voice was in fine shape. The congregation, following his strong lead, sang with more volume than ever. And surely the tones were more mellow. "That's waken th' dead forest," Mrs. Malone whispered to Chris Beth.

Chris Beth smiled and thought ahead to forming the choir that O'Higgin had invited her to help lead. It would be good to sing again—oh, so good. Aunt Mandy used to say in answer to her questions as to why mockingbirds didn't sing in winter, "They's busy storin' up love songs. But best remember, chile, they's music in them silences between." Well, she had been too busy herself this season to practice, too busy serving others. Tomorrow's notes would be sweeter because of the "rests."

"My message will be short," Joe said after the singing. "I want to leave time for testimonials, sharing and real fellowship. Added to prayer, these are the basic ingredients for preparing the heart for dining at the Lord's Table."

The testimonials were so warm and so obviously heart-felt that Chris Beth was sure she cried throughout. The good people praised Joe, Wilson, Vangie, and herself more than she felt they deserved, but, oh, it was so wonderful to be loved and appreciated!

Then came the sharing. "Mostly, folks it's a rehash of what's been promised here afore—the buildin' stuff, man-power, and offerin's that'll hold us together body 'n soul," Nate summed up. "Still 'n all, it's pleasin' to us deacons that yer steadfast!"

Well, now, there was a little more, the attitude of the crowd indicated. Newcomers came forward to rededicate their lives. A couple wanted to dedicate a child to the work of the Lord. And young Wil caused a few smiles and a lot of tears when he stood up tall, brushing at his cowlick, and declared, "I'd like to offer my tree fort to somebody who's been praying for one. I'm too big to use one anymore—and, besides, I've got the upper room here now. I'll even volunteer helpin' to tear it down."

At Vangie's signal, Chris Beth joined her, and the two of them walked toward the improvised altar at the fireplace. Chris Beth paused on the way to squeeze young Wil's hand and then helped her sister move the big package from its hiding place behind the sofa.

"Mrs. Malone!" Startled, Mrs. Malone went forward and, at their urging, opened the heavy wrapping paper from Mama's Christmas present. Velvet—beautiful blue velvet, yards and yards of it—fell into the woman's work-reddened hands.

"To replace your drapes," Vangie said softly. Then, for the first time, Chris Beth saw Mrs. Malone weep.

In the commotion of "oh's" and "ah's," the clearing of throats, and the chorus of blowing noses, Chris Beth was able to slip a large brown envelope onto the altar. Inside was a good sum of cash and a note written after she and Vangie had decided that the brooch had served its purpose—the breaking of one girl's heart and the mending of another. "My donation for roofing a new church," the note read, and there was no signature.

Joe spotted it soon afterward, opened it, and read it aloud. There was a great shout, much like that of the congregation when Joe had buried their worries at sea. And then something more! A little handful of men moved forward, and Chris Beth saw that they were Muslin City folk (only they had cabins now). The youngest man of the group turned to face the guests. "We're donating the piece of ground along the ledge for this new building," he said with clear diction. "And you can count on our lumber and our hands as well."

The second shout was greater than the first. When Chris Beth could hear above the hammering of her heart and force her eyes to focus, Chris Beth realized that yet another miracle was about to occur. Ordinarily, children of the settlement lining up to sing a little off-key song would be just a fitting finale to the worship service. But today the atmosphere was charged with excitement as Joe and then Wilson stepped out to meet the singing group.

Jesus loves the little children,
All the children of the world—

And there their voices stopped. There was pin-drop silence. And what the crowd saw next was unbelievable. As the children finished the little five-line song, Joe and Wilson pointed out a sight that their eyes had never seen before:

Red and yellow, black and white,
All are precious in His sight—

Jesus loves the little children of the world!

Was that real *Indians* coming from between the blackened tree trunk? They asked each other. It had to be. That young buck looked familiar...maybe he was the one Wilson said had volunteered to help them through the winter—"them that could stomach wild sunflower-seed bread and camas-root cake." Yes, they had to be Indians— including a papoose!

Now, the "yellows," was understandable. Seeing as how they'd helped the Chinese and (*ahem!*), yes, the Chus *had* proved to be "above the average." But mercy sakes! Where *did* them "blacks" emerge from? Pretty brave of them, just standing there throughout, singing from that hill yonder. Good voices, too, mellow-like. All surprising—

And I'm the most surprised of all, Chris Beth marveled. *The vision's no longer a dream. It's happening here and now!*

Feeling Joe's gaze, Chris Beth let her eyes meet his. He gave her such a look of naked adoration that she felt her cheeks grown pink. *Oh, Joe*, her eyes signaled back, *I've let go of the past and put our future in the Lord's hands for safekeeping!*

Joe smiled, then stood as if for the benediction. "Thank You, Lord!" Chris Beth said fervently, not caring that her lips moved. "I asked for instant happiness, but You sub-tituted lasting joy!"

Mrs. Malone tried to hurry into the kitchen, undoubtedly to make sure that her girls had laid the table out just right for the Thanksgiving Day feast. But Joe raised a hand to detain her.

"We've found wonderful ways of praising our Maker to-day, but there remains one more." Joe paused, seeming to make eye contact with every person in the large crowd. "It seems only fitting that we allow time for opening our hearts and the doors of our church."

There were several *Amens*. Then Joe said slowly, "One d-day—" Chris Beth, noting his slight stammer, knew that he was about to take a giant step. The others seemed to sense it too. "One day," he continued, his voice gathering strength with each word, "*all* of God's children will be drawn together as He intended—red and yellow, black and white!

Until then, let us draw closer to each other here. I invite anyone wishing to rededicate his life to come, or anyone wishing to make a profession of faith for the first time."

Olga Goldsmith's fingers moved softly over the keys of the old organ. "Just As I Am, Without One Plea—"

Then, except for the moving strains of the old hymn, there was a stunned silence. Surely all breathing had stopped at once. For, with eyes downcast and shoulders slumped forward as if in defeat, Maggie Solomon was slipping down the aisle—hoping, it seemed—to get past unnoticed.

There was a little stir as Joe welcomed the girl. Her voice was almost inaudible as she answered his gentle questions. Chris Beth, sitting so near to the front, was able to hear him tell Maggie that she no longer had anything to be ashamed of—that she could stand tall in her victory—and then he said, "I now offer you the right hand of Christian fellowship."

Maggie turned to face the congregation—or were they her enemies? The next few moments would tell. Chris Beth caught her breath as Vangie deliberately opened her eyes, stood her full height, and prepared to walk the short distance separating her from the other girl. Nobody else, she was certain, heard Vangie's whispered words. "This one's for *you*, Susanah," she said.

Maggie lifted her head almost in fear as Vangie approached. And then her eyes made contact with Vangie's. It wasn't much. Just a glance. And then a handclasp. But maybe it was enough to fan the little spark that had lain in the ashes of Maggie's troubled heart so long. Waiting. Just waiting for love to give it new life.

The crowd surged forward to shake hands with their newest member. Someone rang the great dinnerbell. Wolf gave out a tail-wagging kind of bark as somewhere a lark trilled. The very hills seemed to sing in their silence. And Chris Beth was sure that God in His heaven smiled as He saw His plan fulfilled.

"Bless this hoose!" O'Higgin boomed.

"House!" said Mrs. Mollie O'Higgin Malone.

Dear Reader:

We would appreciate hearing from you regarding the June Masters Bacher Pioneer Romance Series. It will enable us to continue to give you the best in inspirational romance fiction.

Mail to: Pioneer Romance Editors
Harvest House Publishers, 1075 Arrowsmith
Eugene, OR 97402

1. What most influenced you to purchase **LOVE'S SILENT SONG**?
   - ☐ The Christian story
   - ☐ Cover
   - ☐ Backcover copy
   - ☐ _____
   - ☐ Recommendations
   - ☐ Other June Masters Bacher Pioneer Romances you've read

2. Where did you purchase **LOVE'S SILENT SONG**?
   - ☐ Christian bookstore
   - ☐ General bookstore
   - ☐ Other
   - ☐ Grocery store
   - ☐ Department store

3. Your overall rating of this book:
   - ☐ Excellent ☐ Very good ☐ Good ☐ Fair ☐ Poor

4. How many Bacher Pioneer Romances have you read altogether?
   (Choose one) ☐ 1-2 ☐ 3-6 ☐ 7-11 ☐ Over 11

5. How likely would you be to purchase other Bacher Pioneer Romances?
   - ☐ Very likely
   - ☐ Somewhat likely
   - ☐ Not very likely
   - ☐ Not at all

6. Please check the box next to your age group.
   - ☐ Under 18
   - ☐ 18-24
   - ☐ 25-34
   - ☐ 35-39
   - ☐ 40-54
   - ☐ Over 55

Name _____

Address _____

City _____ State _____ Zip _____

Harvest House Publishers

For the Best in Inspirational Fiction

RUTH LIVINGSTON HILL CLASSICS

Bright Conquest
The Homecoming (mass paper)
The South Wind Blew Softly (mass paper)

June Masters Bacher
PIONEER ROMANCE NOVELS

Series 1

1. Love Is a Gentle Stranger
2. Love's Silent Song
3. Diary of a Loving Heart
4. Love Leads Home
5. Love Follows the Heart
6. Love's Enduring Hope

Series 2

1. Journey to Love
2. Dreams Beyond Tomorrow
3. Seasons of Love
4. My Heart's Desire
5. The Heart Remembers
6. From This Time Forth

Series 3

1. Love's Soft Whisper
2. Love's Beautiful Dream
3. When Hearts Awaken
4. Another Spring
5. When Morning Comes Again
6. Gently Love Beckons

HEARTLAND HERITAGE SERIES

No Time for Tears
Songs in the Whirlwind
Where Lies Our Hope
Return to the Heartland

Lori Wick
A PLACE CALLED HOME SERIES

A Place Called Home
A Song for Silas
The Long Road Home
A Gathering of Memories

THE CALIFORNIANS

Whatever Tomorrow Brings
As Time Goes By
Sean Donovan
Donovan's Daughter

THE KENSINGTON CHRONICLES

The Hawk and the Jewel
Wings of the Morning
Who Brings Forth the Wind
The Knight and the Dove

MaryAnn Minatra
THE ALCOTT LEGACY

The Tapestry
The Masterpiece
The Heirloom (Winter 1995)

Lisa Samson
THE HIGHLANDERS

The Highlander and His Lady
The Legend of Robin Brodie

Ellen Traylor
BIBLICAL NOVELS

Esther   Joseph
Moses   Joshua
     Samson

Other Romance Novels

The Hills of God, *Wiggin*